GALAXY OF EMPIRES

Merchant Wars Episode #1

BRUCE ALAN MARCOM

Copyright ©2015 Bruce Alan Marcom
Published by United States Publishing, LLC at Smashwords

http://www.galaxyofempires.com

Smashwords Edition License Notes

This eBook is licensed for your personal enjoyment only. This eBook may not be re-sold or given away to other people. If you would like to share this book with another person, please purchase an additional copy for each recipient. If you're reading this book and did not purchase it, or it was not purchased for your enjoyment only, then please return to Smashwords.com or your favorite retailer and purchase your own copy. Thank you for respecting the hard work of this author.

ISBN: 1943917035
ISBN: 9781943917037

US Copyright 1-2781753491

Table of Contents

Chapter 1	1
Chapter 2	8
Chapter 3	21
Chapter 4	27
Chapter 5	42
Chapter 6	56

Chapter 1

Evella Noctu, carrying her electronic accounting pad, walked briskly down the hall. She was trying to get to the conference room in her cruiser before the other captains arrived. They had just landed on the reptilian home world of Hosan at her home base of operations. As she came up to the conference room door, she saw her assistant, 42, standing there and waiting for her. Her assistant was a tall android with a highly polished and blackened chrome paint job.

Being a reptilian merchant was not only a dangerous job but trust is also one thing that never exists—at least among reptilian merchants. Eve never believes anyone, particularly because she is a half-breed: part human and part snake. That was one of the reasons she decided to get an android assistant instead of using a biological one. Besides, it is unlikely that any reptilian could keep up with the accounting better than an android, not to mention the fact that it is also unlikely that an android would ever betray her unless the android had been tampered with.

"Is everything ready, 42?"

"Yes, My Lady, I have all the records in order and available for review for the meeting."

"Excellent. Your efficiency never ceases to amaze me, 42, even after all these years."

"Thank you, Ma'am. I try to do the best I can." The android, in a humble fashion, says, "There is one thing I would like to bring to your attention...."

There are some irregularities with one of the captain's records; he appears to be short on one of his accounts."

Eve responds with interest, "Oh, really? Let me see the records you are referring to and we shall see what the captain has been up to." She grabs the accounting pad and scans it with scrutiny. After a few minutes, she looks up at 42 and says, "You are correct, of course, and this will have to be dealt with. I want you to follow these instructions closely." She gives 42 some instructions.

⯅

"Order, order. Take your seats, captains, and let us get on with this. I do not have all day." Eve barks with a loud tone to get everyone's attention as she glared at all the reptilian captains.

"Now the first thing on the agenda is last month's profit goals. Everything seems to be in order following a very profitable month last month. Capt. Bly had the highest profit margins out of all six ships in our fleet with raw minerals being at the top of the list." The captains begin clapping in recognition of this achievement.

42 speaks: "The following is the list of profit margin by each captain: Capt. Bly in our minerals division had a profit margin of 42.0%; Capt. Kuhn in our arts and crafts division had 39.5%; Capt. Fujima in our food division had 21.3%; Capt. Jezikar in the small arms division had 37%; Capt. Terinad in the ship weapons, armor, and shield generators division had 36.9%, and Capt. Bloodtail in our smuggling department had 39.4%."

"As Bly, Kuhn, and Bloodtail exceeded their projections, they are the only ones who get bonuses this month," Eve remarks with contentment. "Capt. Fujima, your production level has been disappointing these past three months. You should be making a killing with the famine in sector three. You could have easily charged three times the average price for food because those starving people would have paid anything for it."

Capt. Fujima replies nervously, "There has been a lot of competition, not just me, and the Buscar Merchant clan is one of the biggest food distributors in the region, which makes it hard for me to compete with them."

Eve says with a commanding voice, "A good merchant can always make a profit under any circumstance. Instead, you make excuses. However, what I am concerned about is your inventory, which was audited as was your bookkeeping. The audit discovered that you are missing two full ship containers of food. I had those containers tracked and found that you gave free food to those starving children."

The other captains gasp when they hear the word free. A reptilian merchant giving away merchandise is the most forbidden taboo in the merchant industry, and it is a good way to get a merchant license revoked permanently in addition to incurring fines and penalties.

"I...they were starving.... I felt sorry for them...," Capt. Fujima sobs.

"You are a disgrace to reptilians everywhere. You know what the penalties are for giving away merchandise. There will be no leniency whatsoever. The merchants' guild has given me the power to strip you of your merchant and pilot licenses. In addition to the merchant guild's penalties, your employment contract with me states that any captain is to be held liable if he loses merchandise because of negligence, theft, destruction, or any other reason. The employer, which is me, can exercise the right to liquidate all of the employee's assets to recover the losses incurred by the employee."

"What? But...," Fujima shrieks, but he is cut off.

"And since you like to work for free, I have arranged for you to work free for the remainder of your life."

Two large crocodile men in leather armor with whips and handcuffs attached to their belts walk in the room and approach Capt. Fujima and grab him. "These two fine gentlemen are from the slavers' guild because I have sold you to them to help compensate me for my losses. Since that was not enough to cover all of your debts, the rest of your assets have been liquidated as well. Unfortunately, that still was not sufficient, so I had a sell your wife and children into slavery."

As the captain struggles with the large crocodile men who are handcuffing him, he yells out, "You half-breed piece of crap! I will kill you if it is the last thing I do...." The crocodile men start to drag him out of the room, but suddenly stop when Eve sternly says in an angry tone, "What did you call me…?"

The other captains start backing away from the offender who was getting up off the floor. The last time somebody used the "H-word" in reference to Eve, that person's head exploded from the inside out. The word half-breed used in a negative tone is the most offensive word anyone could say to her.

Eve stands up from the table and extends her hand as if trying to grab Fujima. An invisible force hoists the captain up into the air where he begins to choke and violently thrashes around trying to breathe. Eve is a telepath and a powerful one at that.

"You are in no position to threaten anyone, Captain. I did not just sell your wife into slavery, I sold her to a brothel that needed someone to give freebies to all of their new clients as a sample of their services. Just think of all those satisfied customers who will get to sample your wife for free. But then again, she will probably get more satisfaction from them than from you."

"The slavers' guild would not take your newborn baby. Therefore, I had to go and try to sell your new baby on the adoption market. However, on the way over there, I ran across a human who said he would offer me twice as much as the adoption market would. He said that he needed some food for his dragon lizard pet and the baby would be perfect. So I sold the baby to him and watched the dragon lizard devour your little gremlin until it was gone."

She releases the captain and he falls to the floor, gasping for air. She starts to turn around and sit in her chair, but stops and says in an even tone, "Screw the money…." As her eyes light up with a blue glow, suddenly the captain's head explodes from inside out as the mind blast completes its effect.

"Take note, Captains. I do not take kindly to people who betray or insult me. In contrast, I reward those who respect me and are productive. After all, we are all in this to make money. Do not get sidetracked by becoming too greedy or not staying focused on the objectives I have laid out. Dismissed." The captains leave the room in a hurried fashion, as none wanted to be the target of her wrath.

"Sorry, gentlemen, for making you waste a trip, but I tell you what, I will give you a hundred platinum bars to dispose of this mess so at least you'll get something out of it." The sound of platinum bars makes the slavers happy, so they began to clean up what was left of Capt. Fujima on the floor.

"On second thought, put the meat in the frozen box that my assistant will get for you. I will feed the captain to my giant snake later tonight." She walks out of the room and back to her private chamber.

⁂

A few days have passed since the captains' monthly meeting. Eve is checking the inventory on her ship to make sure that it is correct and on time, as well as loaded correctly in the cargo hold.

"My Lady, we should be ready to leave in the next 30 minutes or so. Everything is loaded. We have approximately 50 containers of food and are ready to go to sector three. We will have to make up for the loss of a captain," 42 states. Eve opens up one of the crates to check it and sees giant rats eating the food in the container. Looks like most of the food is either half eaten or spoiled in that container.

"Who sold us these containers and why were they not checked at first before we received them?" Eve growls.

"By the late Capt. Fujima, of course, and we got them from Capt. Iquzel, a merchant from the Pirate Lord's territory."

"That is the second time that sack of dung has sold me bad goods. I am going inside and contact his boss." She walks out of the cargo hold into the corridor and passes several doors in the hallway before she arrives at her office. She speaks on the vid screen and says, "Connect me to Lord Cos." A large, hairy, black male Wolfkin appears on the screen.

"Lady Evella, how's business? Everything okay over there in the lizard land?"

"I am a snake, not a lizard, but I know we all look the same to you. But to answer your question, my business would be better if your merchants would stop selling me bad goods. Also, this is the second time the same dealer has sold me bad goods: Capt. Iquzel."

"Oh, goodness, let me pull the shipping manifest. Ah, here we go, hmm, looks like Capt. Fujima signed off on the shipment. You know I would never sell you bad stuff intentionally. That is why we require all shipments to be inspected first before we release them. Nevertheless, in the interest of continued business relations, I will look into this thoroughly and see if there are any irregularities. I do not want my good name being tarnished."

His good name? He is a freaking pirate, Eve thinks to herself. "I am out 5,000 platinum bars, not to mention the profit I could have made. I demand some sort of compensation for this travesty," she says, clearly running out of patience with the whole matter.

"Like I said, My Lady, I will look into it, I assure you. Just give me a couple of days, and I will contact you as soon as possible."

"Very well, vid off," Eve curses, "Even in death, Fujima is still screwing me over. Too bad I can only kill him once…." She mumbles some obscenities and continues down the corridor toward the cargo bay.

"So what is the damage?" Eve inquires.

42 gets out a checklist, "Well, it is not all spoiled as there are about 20 containers of good food that we can sell for 6,000 platinum bars. The other 30 containers are all spoiled and have rats in them. And I hate rats…disgusting creatures." The Android pulls out his hand blaster and fires. The shot hits a rat, making it explode in a midair jump.

"Okay, take all the rats and put them into two containers and ship them to the pet food vendors on Ganalag. You should be able to get 400 platinum bars easy. Ship the other 28 containers of bad food to the planet Extek. There is a fertilizer company that will give me 100 platinum bars for each container of bad food."

"Wow, those are good ideas, Boss. I would never think of that, but then again, that is why you are the boss. I will 'volunteer' someone else to gather up the rats," 42 says with some awe.

"Yep, heh, check the shipping schedules of our captains and see which ones can take which containers, depending on what direction they are going, and that way we can cut our shipping cost down as much as possible. And then…." Eve suddenly pauses without reason and just stands there with a blank expression on her face, not moving. An eerie voice begins speaking to Eve telepathically.

"I am Dracabardillious; you must travel to three-way border of the 8, 3, 1 junction now before it is too late."

"Boss…Boss…are you there?" The cargo hold supervisor says frantically.

Eve snaps out of the mild trance and says, "Yes, just follow the instructions I gave." She looks at 42 and says, "Tell me when all this stuff is offloaded. Make flight plans for the neutral zone, and we will take off in an hour."

42 is confused at this remark and says, "Uh…huh? What about our shipping schedule? Neutral Zone? We're taking off with no merchandise loaded?" But Eve has already left and gone into the ship.

Chapter 2

"Is the pre-flight check done yet?" Eve inquires.

"Yes, and I also loaded 20 type-E mines, a status web net, and the cloaking device you requested. I am not sure the cloaking device will work on our ship because of its size. The device was created for smaller ships like fighters or shuttles and our ship is the size of a Class 3 destroyer. We do have three shuttles in the cargo bay," 42 informs.

"That is fine. I want to do a weapons check when we are in orbit and before we take off to the destination. I want all the weapons tested, including the large projectile cannons, medium pulse lasers, and the small rotating guns. Make sure we have missiles at maximum capacity for all of our missile racks," Eve says insistently.

"We're going to war or something? Geez that is a lot of firepower," 42 ponders.

"I just like to be ready for anything that might come up, especially in an area that is unpredictable and unstable as a neutral zone. Also make sure all 197 crew members are ready to go."

"Why are we going out in the middle of nowhere, might I ask?"

"You may not. Just trust me, 42. I would never do anything that would jeopardize any of our lives or my ship—you should know that by now. I just want to go and check something out."

"Okay, Boss. You know, I always have faith in you. You are probably one of the smartest persons I have ever met. I enjoy working for you, not just for the money, or all the upgrades that I have gotten for my body, but you have an active mind and are sagacious for your years."

"Okay, stop kissing the boss's butt, 42, and come up to the bridge. I am having an issue with the tactical display at the weapons station," Gartooth Hammertail says in an unimpressed fashion while standing in the cargo bay door halfway in the main corridor. 42 turns around and sees the huge crocodile man with the protruding jawline and crooked teeth leaning against the door frame with his arms crossed. "Well, chop, chop, let's go. I ain't got all day, got things to do, people to kill and such...."

"You know you are the most annoying person I have ever met," 42 grumbles and heads up to the bridge with Gartooth. Eve giggles a little; watching those to work together is somewhat of a comedy relief sometimes. Gartooth has been the tactical officer on the ship for three years and sometimes he can be annoying but knows his job very well. He comes from a crocodile family that mostly had security job careers over the last century or so.

The rest of the crew is a motley bunch of interesting characters. At the helm is Helma Seni, a snake female with her twin sister, Nelma Seni, at navigation. Then, of course, there is 42, who is an android, in charge of communications and accounting. Rulu Barbtail, a female crocodile, is the chief engineer. Meto Shawn, a human male, is the first officer and controls the science station and sensor ops. Dr. Farshe Mezeenabark, a female Wolfkin, is the ship's chief medical officer. Pura Shitztar, cargo supervisor and ship's cook, is a female Katlin (cat people).

Eve goes back to her office to attend to some last-minute details before they launch. As she sits in her chair, the vid screen starts beeping, indicating an incoming call. She presses a button, and a snake man appears on the screen.

"Hello, Lady Eve. I heard you were back in Hoshan. How does it feel to be back home?" Fartan Balltail asks politely to his favorite client. Fartan is the attorney for Eve's merchant group and has been for about three years. His specialty is corporate law. In this case, the lawyer is literally a snake and not just figuratively.

"What's up, Fartan? I am just getting ready to take off in a few minutes."

"I just called to inform you that the merchant group Digtailan has just declared war on your merchant group. I got the notice from the merchant guild today. Digtailan paid all the appropriate filing fees with the merchant guild, so it is an official war."

"I thought they were a Class Eight merchant like me. How can they challenge the same rank? I thought the challenger had to challenge one rank above their own rank."

"You can challenge the same rank as long as the combined total of both groups' assets equal enough to qualify the winner for the next rank's license. For example, both contestants are rank eight and their combined total assets equal enough value to apply for a Class Seven license."

"Oh well, that sucks big time, as we are already fighting two other corporations. Guess we will just add them to the list. It is bad enough we have to fight off the companies below us and now we have to worry about companies with the same rank as ours. Getting tired of this crap. I guess I will have to take out one or two of these challengers to show them not to screw with me. The higher the ranked license, the bigger the contracts, and the more money my company makes." This is why the reptilian merchant ships are also warships. They do not fear pirates, who would never attack a reptilian merchant ship because those ships are far better armed, armored, and shielded than any pirate ship. Reptilian merchant ships double as warships because the fighting among them is more dangerous than anything else they might encounter.

"I will send a message out to my other ships to add that group to the list of attack-on-sight ships." She presses a button that transmits a message to her fleet.

A few minutes later, she activates the ship-wide intercom and informs, "Attention all crew members. We will be disembarking in approximately 30 minutes. Make sure all of your tasks have been completed and that you are at your action stations and ready for takeoff at 13:00 hours." About that time, she hears her door chime. "Enter."

A tall, slender, black-and-white, tiger-striped female Katlin in pink shorts and a pink tank top walks in the office carrying a box on a dolly and another thin rectangular package.

"This just came for you," Pura Shitztar stated simply. She sets the box on the desk.

"Thank you, Pura." Eve gets up and begins to open the box. Pura shrieks at the sight of the box's contents. Eve pulls out the severed head of a snake man, which appears to be the head of Capt. Iquzel. There is a note attached to the side of the box, which Eve detaches as she put the head back in the box. She reads the letter aloud:

My Lady, I am sorry my former employee has caused you inconveniences. I hope that this small token will make amends for any loss that you may have incurred. I hope to continue our business relationship, as you are one of the best customers I have. Please take these two gifts as a token of my appreciation for your business. May your profits always be high, My Lady. Signed, Lord Cos.

"That is so gross; I think I am going to hurl...." Pura leaves the room in a rush to get to the nearest bathroom. Eve just sits there and smiles while thinking to herself, *I have just the place for this head.* She presses a button on her desk and a side panel opens. There are a couple of rows of heads mounted on the wall.

"Yes, this will go nicely in my head collection. I will have to polish it up first and then it will go great right here," she says as she checks an open slot for the head size of her new trophy. This head would be the first in her collection that was not one of her own victims. She opens up the other package, which appears to be a painting of herself done by a very famous reptilian artist named Yuha Jukuna. "Oh my, look at this picture of me by Yuha Jukuna that must have cost a fortune. Looks like Lord Cos is flirting with me with these gifts. Vid screen on." The screen becomes active. "Lord Cos, please."

"Well hello, Lady Eve," the Wolfkin says with anticipation.

"I just received your gifts. You sure know how to charm a girl. Thank you so much. I am very pleased to say the least."

"I am happy to hear our relationship has not been damaged. I am glad you enjoyed the gifts. I look forward to our next transaction."

"Indeed, so do I. I will chat with you later as I am about to take off. I just wanted you to know that I received the gifts and to let you know all is well with us. May profits guide you and your ventures. Good day, vid out."

The intercom activates once again for an incoming message.

"Boss, we are ready to take off. Are you coming up to the bridge?" 42 asks.

"Yes, I am coming up there now."

▲

On the bridge, the crew is waiting for the captain before initiating the takeoff and conducting last-minute checks at the same time.

"Just daydreaming about being the meat in between two fine-looking twin snake babes…," Gartooth says snidely with a grin and chuckle.

Meto interjects, "Thank you for the mental picture that will cause me a few weeks of mental therapy to get it out of my head."

"Not even if I was drunk and passed out, Gar," snaps Helma as she blows on the fresh nail polish she recently applied to her long nails.

Helma's twin sister, Nelma, adds," I would rather get a root canal than sleep with you, Gartooth, not to mention all the disinfectant I would need to purify my room after you left."

They all begin laughing. The twin snake women were the navigator and helm control for the ship. For both young ladies, this was their first merchant tour.

"Har, Har, don't knock it till you try it, Sugar Cakes," Gartooth flails his tongue at the twins.

"That is truly disgusting. No wonder you do not have a girlfriend. I do not even think female crocodiles would be interested in you," Helma says with an unpleasant look on her face.

Eve walks onto the bridge and sits in the captain's chair.

"Captain on deck" the first officer announces.

"Alright folks, time to go. Helma contact the tower and let us get it out of here."

Helma presses a button, "Control tower this is the merchant vessel *Evella* requesting clearance for takeoff."

"*Evella*, proceed to takeoff platform seven and wait for further instructions from the control tower."

"Affirmative, control tower. En route now."

"Evella, proceed to ignition; takeoff in 30 seconds."

"Here we go.... Takeoff in 10, nine, eight, seven, six, five, four, three, two, one.... Activating lift-off burners, and here we go...," Helma continues, "Reaching orbit in 63 seconds."

"Course set for the neutral zone, Boss," informs Nelma.

"FTL engines online and ready for jump, Boss," states Helma.

"Proceed," Eve commands. The ship zips off into space to its destination.

"We should reach the neutral zone in approximately five days."

"Thank you, Nelma. Keep me informed of any changes by the head office. Meto, you have the com." Eve leaves the bridge and walks down the hallway to the lift doors and waits for the turbo lift. After getting to her office, she sits at her desk and brings up her computer screen and says, "Computer, do a search and display all data on Empress Draca."

"Query found. Empress Draca is known as Dracabardillous and other names in different parts of the galaxy. This entity is of unknown origin, unknown race, and unknown age, though some speculate that she is thousands or even millions of years old. Some believe the entity is an energy being with immense power. The entity is the creator of the machine people and the Consortium Empire. The entity has been described as having godlike telepathic abilities able to communicate with artificial intelligence (AI) beings or telepaths anywhere in the galaxy at any time. The entity usually inhabits an android body that has the shape of a human female. No other androids have bodies that resemble other biological creatures. The entity has been known to inhabit multiple bodies at the same time, and all of them have the similar incarnation of a female human body. The exact size of the Consortium's Empire is unknown, but it is vast and covers multiple galaxies. The entity's true goals are unknown, but it does have an interest in telepaths and AI beings. Some scholars suspect this entity created telepaths and spread them across the universe. End query."

Eve wonders why such a powerful being would contact her and send her a message. It has been bothering her ever since it happened. *What does all this mean? she ponders. It must have something to do with telepaths or telepathy.*

⚴

"Captain, we have made contact with another ship, so you might want to get up here," 42 says with urgency over the intercom.

"On my way." A few minutes later, Eve appears on the bridge and sits in her chair.

"Report."

"It's the transport ship *Endure*. Looks like they have about 50 passengers and some laser blast damage.... They have been shot up pretty bad," Meto reports.

"That your boyfriend's ship, Boss," Helma says.

"He is not my boyfriend. He is just a good friend," Eve says solemnly.

The *Endure* smuggles telepaths out of the Elemental Empire where telepaths are illegal. Once in reptilian space, the ship takes them to the capital where there is a Consortium embassy. Telepath refugees are given citizenship and shipped some off to Consortium space. The Consortium Empire welcomes all telepaths unconditionally by decree of Empress Draca.

"On vid," Eve says. A human male in his 30s with blonde hair and blue eyes appears on the screen.

"Greetings, Captain Eve. How is the most beautiful snake lady in the universe doing today? Profits up?" Captain Zach Blem says in a flirting manner.

Eve smiles and blushes while subconsciously primping her hair, "Hi, Capt. Blem. Looks like you have taken a beaten by those nasty telepath police. Are you in need of assistance?"

"Well, we could use some parts and maybe borrow one of your mechanics for a bit. Some food will help out as well, if you don't mind; we got a lot of starving refugees."

"We got plenty of food over here. We can give you a few crates, and my mechanics can lend assistance for a while. But it is going to cost you…dinner over here with me."

"You drive a hard bargain, Captain. 16:00 okay?"

"That is fine."

Zach sends a telepathic message, "I miss you a lot."

"Hurry up and get your human butt over here, and do not keep me waiting, Tiger," Eve answers telepathically.

Vid ends.

"Your friend, huh? Your eyes are popping out of your head, and if you blush any more, you gonna match your red sweater," Helma pokes fun.

"He is exquisite looking for a human. I am already trying to picture what my half-human babies would look like," Nelma giggles.

"He is definitely a hottie, that is for sure," Helma says.

"Bah, you need a real male with big muscles like a crocodile man, not one of those skinny humans," Gartooth objects.

"Hey, I am a human," Meto exclaims, flexing his arm muscles.

"Yeah, but you are no Capt. Blem with those blues eyes and yellow hair," Nelma says with a dreamy look. The twins start to giggle in unison.

"Well, Meto, you have the com. I have to go and check on getting those food supplies ready," Eve says in a hurried manner.

"More like getting ready for stud muffin to come over," Nemla winks at Eve." "I don't blame you. I would be hitting the beauty salon about now getting in a good turtle wax on my scales if he were my date."

"We are just friends…," Eve rolls her eyes with a glowing smile and heads out the door.

"More like friends with benefits…," Gartooth chuckles. They all burst out laughing.

⅄

Two hours pass, and Eve and Zach have just entered her quarters. They sit down at a small round table with two chairs on both sides. There is a nicely prepared and organized meal for two on the table. A large vase with blue flowers sits off to the right of the couple.

"This meal looks just as ravishing as you do, Darling," Zach says in a seductive fashion.

Eve blushes and replies, "Thank you. You are such a charmer." She winks at Zach.

"I made an ancient Earth recipe called 'pizza.' I don't have much experience with human food because I do not meet too many humans out in these parts. I know that Earth is an old planet that is not habitable anymore. Elemental Empire conquered it thousands of years ago, but surprisingly there are relatively good records of what it was like before the sun burned out."

"I am not much of a history buff, but most of the records about human origination, I think, are probably a fabrication of the Elemental Empire government. They are excellent at fabricating information that makes them look good," Zach advises. "I know it is a touchy subject with you, but I am kind of curious at how you are half-human and half-snake as I did not think they were compatible races. But if the subject is uncomfortable for you, we do not have to talk about it."

"Well, it is an uncomfortable subject, but I will tell you what I know. I think I was created in a laboratory from what I can vaguely remember. I was being transported as a child from this place I can barely remember and pirates attacked the ship. The pirates killed the crew, but decided to sell me into slavery probably because I was a child. A snake merchant bought me, even though his wife objected because I was a half-breed. They wanted to adopt a child, but because they were so old, they could not use the regular adoption methods of the Reptilian Empire. Therefore, this couple went to see if they could buy a child slave and adopt instead. Unfortunately, there are very few child slaves as most of them go to the adoption Guild."

"After this old snake merchant couple bought me, I stayed aboard the ship most of the time as the captain's girl. I did all the errands and stuff that he wanted me to do. After a few years passed, his wife grew attached to me and eventually urged her husband to adopt me officially. It was kind of hard because I had no birth certificate, but most slaves do not have papers—nothing a few platinum bars could not fix. I grew attached to them and considered them as my parents, even though they were not my biological parents. My father only had one ship and a class 10 merchant's license when he died. My adoptive mother died soon thereafter, mainly of a broken heart. I inherited what little they had, which included one beat-up merchant ship. Today, I have seven merchant war cruisers in my fleet and a class 8 merchant license with about 2,000 people working for me."

"That is an impressive feat considering where you came from. My story is more boring than yours. My family disowned me when they learned I was a telepath because of all the propaganda and telepath-related hatred in the Elemental Empire. My parents turned me over to the authorities as soon as I started displaying telepathic abilities when I was 15 or so. Unlike regular telepaths, my abilities far exceeded those of most telepaths."

"I got to the concentration camp, and they separated me from the other telepaths and started taking blood samples along with conducting other kinds of tests on me. They were going to ship me off to some special secret laboratory that I overheard them talking about. However, I escaped during the transport attempt. I used my telepathic abilities to survive because my abilities were high enough that they bypassed all of the telepathic defenses set up by the government. For example, those telepathic metal helmets the police use for defense against telepathic powers do not work against my abilities. Therefore, you can imagine every time the police tried to arrest me, I would just plant suggestions in their heads and they would stand there staring out into space while I escaped. I wanted to stay off the radar, so I did not kill anybody because that would draw attention to me. It much easier just to escape and hide."

"I guess we are both hard cases then," Eve acknowledges as she resumes eating.

Zach continues," I am happy that I met you. I think that you being a half-breed makes you different, even unique. I think your snakeskin mixed in with your human skin makes you more attractive, at least to me. I am glad that you are a telepath as well, which makes it even better. Your PSI rating must be equal to mine or even higher. Do you know how strong your PSI rating is?

Have you ever had it tested? Mine is 18 on the 20 scale. Most telepaths are 1–15."

"I am not sure and I never really thought about it. I never have anything to compare it to. I haven't had much contact with other telepaths, except for you. On the other hand, I should say I never socialized with another telepath. I have encountered some telepaths, but mostly in passing."

"Well, if you are curious, I have a PSI tester with me."

"I am curious, not that it matters to me even if it is low."

"Even if it is low, that does not mean anything—you are still a telepath. But you might be stronger than you think and you don't now because you have never been tested."

After all the plates and glasses are cleared off, Zach pulls out an electronic device and puts it on the table. He pulls out five cylinders, each a different size and width.

"Okay, this machine will register your PSI strength. What I want you to do is crush each of these cylinders one at a time."

Eve focuses on the first one and bends it very easily. The second cylinder is a bit harder, but she bends it very easily as well. The third cylinder is getting harder to bend, but Eve does it without too much effort. The fourth cylinder is considerably harder to bend and takes her a few moments. Then she starts on the fifth cylinder, which is massive and extremely difficult to bend. She focuses all of her energy and thoughts on crushing it and eventually it begins to turn slowly. Eve is sweating very profusely on her face and forehead. The cylinder starts making a creaking noise as it slowly, but steadily, bends into an L-shape. Zach looks on with amazement as he had never seen *anyone* bend the fifth cylinder, not even himself. Eve grunts and the cylinder becomes red hot and melts on the table and disintegrates into hot metal drops all over the table.

"Wow, you have really strong telepathic abilities! I have never seen that before or even heard of anyone who has ever done that. The machine says 20 PSI, but it only goes up to 20, so you may be more than 20, if there is such a thing," Zach says with amazement.

"Interestingly, I did not know," Eve says, trying to recover from the strain. She thought to herself: *This is very useful information, especially when it comes to dealing with my enemies. Not bad for being a lab experiment.*

"You need to spend more time with other telepaths to increase your knowledge and experience with your telepathic abilities. You probably have some abilities that you are not aware of. The only way that you can ever fully appreciate them is with other telepaths. You have probably mastered telekinesis, telepathy, and suggestion. Most telepathic people start with those because they are the most common abilities. Have you tried energy projection or invisibility?"

"Um...no. I did not even know I could do that."

"You probably can and a lot more. I will show you what I can do. I have never known anyone who had a PSI rating higher than I do. You may have other abilities beyond known telepathic abilities. I suggest you take a trip to the Consortium and access their telepathic library, which is probably the most comprehensive as far as telepathic studies. The person you really need to talk to is Empress Draca, if that is even possible. Draca is not known for speaking to people outside of the Consortium. In fact, she rarely talks with anyone, even within the Consortium."

"Really...hmm," Eve becomes concerned about the message Empress Draca sent her, and then realizes she is with a guest right now.

Zach says, "Hold your hand out and picture holding a fireball. Focus on that."

Eve gently puts her hand forth and looks at it. She begins focusing on that thought for a few seconds as her hand ignites with fire. Then she starts to make different shapes with the fire in her hand, such as turning her hand to the wall and shooting the flame into the wall and igniting it. The ship-wide intercom comes on, blaring, "Warning! Fire in the Captain's quarters! Warning! Fire in the Captain's quarters! This is not a drill!"

"Woah there, Girl on Fire," Zach says loudly. "You need to watch it there before you burn us up. You can also put it out, but that is usually with water and not with your mind." They both laughed as they grab the fire extinguisher hanging on the wall. About that time, the door chimes and someone asks, "Captain, are you okay in there?"

Eve says, "It is all good. The fire is out. Return to your station."

"You need to start small and work your way up, Princess. You can also do that with electricity—but not tonight. We don't need any more fires, ha-ha."

Eve giggles.

"Now when two telepaths make love, it is very different than when non-telepaths do it. All of the senses are amplified. The more powerful the telepaths, the more intense the sexual encounter. Now…do you want to find out if half-breeds can be made outside the lab…?" Zach says with a big grin and a wink.

Eve chuckles, "But, of course. Let's play Doctor.…"

Chapter 3

The next day the *Endure* went on its way to the capital with its host of telepaths. Eve had set a course to the neutral zone and went on her way. By the fourth day, the trip had been uneventful up to that time. Now they had left Reptilian space and were entering the neutral zone. Eve had been practicing several new telepathic abilities that she had learned from Zach for the past four days and was mastering them at a very quick pace.

She is sitting in her office when she hears the door chime.

"Enter."

The door opens, and suddenly a blasting sound shrieks into the room for a few moments and then silence. The first officer is standing in the doorway slightly in the room with a blaster pointed at the Captain. He activates the sonic inhibitor that lets out a loud noise on a certain frequency that incapacitates a telepath's telepathic abilities. He fires his blaster at Eve at point blank range. The blaster makes a clicking noise.

Eve remarks, "Oops, looks like your blaster's warranty is up." With her blue eyes flaring, she grabs him and slams him into the wall.

"You did not think it was going to be that easy, did you? I am not an idiot. Are you wondering why your blaster doesn't work or your sonic inhibitor for that matter? It is called an EMP, an electromagnetic pulse. I carry a device around with me that generates a small EMP. My office is equipped with one, too. I have them set to the same frequency that sonic inhibitors use. Therefore, when a sonic inhibitor goes off, it triggers an EMP that kills all the electronics within 50 feet of me or my office. You seriously must be stupid to think I did not have a defense against sonic inhibitors. People try to kill me all the time. Thus, I have defenses in place."

"While you are struggling on the floor to breathe for air, I am trying to decide whether I want to choke you to death, burn you, or kill you in some other fashion." She presses a button and a panel opens. Her collection of heads gleams as the power reactivates in the room. She probes his mind to see who he is working for.

"So they offered you my ship in return for assassinating me. Once I take out the Apel Merchant Group, I will show them your head that will be filling that empty spot right there on the end of row 2." She takes a huge cleaver out of her desk and walks over to her first officer and lifts him off the ground with telekinesis as he gags for air. She heats up the cleaver with her mind until it glows red-hot and takes a sudden but swift swing, removing Meto's head. She then walks over and places it on the empty peg on row 2 of her heads. *My taxidermist is going to appreciate my business this month for sure*, she thought to herself with a slight giggle.

She presses the intercom button, "42, you are now First Officer. Congratulations. Also, have a custodian come down here in the clean up what is left of our former First Officer. I will be up on the bridge in a few minutes so have a status report ready. Out."

Eve walks down a corridor to get to the bridge when she hears someone behind her chanting, and just as she turns around, she sees a flash of lightning in the corner of her eye. She ducks and rolls to the left with blinding speed as the lightning bolt barely misses her right shoulder and slams into the corridor wall. "Shield," she says as her personal shield activates just in time to intercept another lightning bolt. In front of her is a human female sorcerer wearing a red dress in a black cloak with black hair and green eyes. The sorcerer begins casting through what appeared to be some sort of magical shield. At the same time, another sorcerer from behind her, a human male dressed in black leather, begins casting a spell. Eve realizes she has been caught in an ambush. Both of them are wearing metallic telepathic protection helmets.

"Disintegrate," the female sorcerer says, completing her spell as a red beam shoots out of the hand of the sorcerer and hits Eve's force field. Eve becomes defenseless as her shield drops.

"Lightning," the male sorcerer says as a bolt roars through the air and catches Eve on the left side of her rib cage and she rolls to the right of the hallway. Severely wounded, she knows she is doomed, boxed in like an animal on safari. She hears the sorceress began casting again. She turns her fear into anger stands up slowly holding her left side, which was bleeding out. She focuses her mind, grabs both assassins at the same time, and hoists them up in the air while choking them.

"Hard to cast spells when you can't talk, witches," Eve says in pain. "You like lightning so much, let me give you some of mine." Both her hands began to glow as a huge arc of lightning slams into both airborne figures sending them flying down the hall into the wall. She hits them again, this time maintaining lightning streaks until nothing is left of the bodies except charred remains. As the smoldering corpses release the smoky whispers of burning flesh, Eve walks down the corridor toward the bodies.

"I guess only skulls are left from these two for my collection, heh." She coughs and limps off toward the infirmary.

Over the intercom, an automated message begins playing, "Intruder alert on Deck 13, Section 8, intruder alert on Deck 13, Section 8." Security comes down the hall about the time Eve starts limping toward the infirmary, and she collapses in the hallway just as they arrive.

Gartooth commands, "Secure the corridor door, men. I don't want anyone coming down here unless they are medical personnel." He clicks a button on his com badge, "Farshe, get a medical team down to Deck 13, Section 8 because the boss has been hit really bad. Also, fire crew get your butts down here fast and contain this fire." A few moments later, the medical crew arrives with Dr. Farshe.

"Get her on the gurney and get to the medical bay. Start scans and tests as soon as we get there. I need to prep for surgery. Do it now!" Dr. Farshe barks loudly. They load Eve on the gurney and rush down the hall with the security team following them looking for unknown assassins who may potentially jump out along the way.

Gartooth says on the ship-wide intercom, "The ship is on lockdown; all personnel who are not on duty report to your quarters and stay there. I don't want anybody roaming around while there might be unknown assassins lurking about. If you are not in your room, you will be shot on sight and we will ask questions later if you are still alive. This lockdown is in effect until further notice, Gartooth out." When it comes to security, Gartooth takes his job very seriously and this is one of the reasons Eve recruited him. This is not the first time someone has taken a shot at the Captain, and it will not be the last.

"The trauma team is ready to operate, Doctor."

"Very well, let me see the chart pads for the test results. Okay, looks like some broken ribs and third-degree burns on the left side. Let us get all these clothes off and remove the burnt material from the skin first and disinfect the area."

After about three hours, the doctor completes the surgery. The command staff had been waiting in the sitting area outside the surgery room. The doctor walks outside the hall and notices the twins, Hemla and Semla, pacing back and forth. Gartooth is standing at the doorway along with some security guards placed all around the hallway as well as the waiting room. He had ordered a ship-wide search for any other intruders who were not listed on the ship's manifest of employees. Rulu, the chief engineer, and Pura, the ship's cook and cargo supervisor, were sitting in the chairs waiting for news.

"The surgery was successful. She is not out of the woods yet, but she is stable and very lucky. If she makes it through the night, she should be okay. But you know the Captain—she is stubborn and relentless," the doctor concludes.

"Thank you Dr. Farshe," Hemla says with gratitude.

"Get some rest, guys, and I will inform you if there is any change. There are plenty of security personnel here."

The next morning, 42 goes to check on Eve after his shift on the bridge. He arrives in the infirmary and sees Helma and Nelma sitting on both sides of Eve's bed. Eve is sitting up with some pillows sporting her back and she is talking to the twins. 42 walks up to Eve.

"Boss, you gave us a real scare there," 42 says.

"I will survive. Just got caught with my pants down so to speak. I am more embarrassed they caught me in an ambush unprepared. Any idea who the assassins were or should I say which one of my enemies sent them?"

"From what we can tell, they came aboard one of the shuttles from *Endure* that was picking up the supplies that you were sending to them. They pretended to be members of the Endure's crew. Nobody noticed them not getting back on the shuttles when they left. Unfortunately, there was not much left of their bodies after you are finished with them, Boss. New abilities I presume? Not that I mind, it just means that my favorite boss will be sticking around a lot longer than my previous bosses because they were weaker. Did find metal tags on them, and it looks like they were possibly spies for the telepathic police from the Elemental Empire. My guess is they thought you were part of the telepathic underground movement and were trying to take you out."

"Makes sense. I guess I am on their hit list now. I was not expecting an assassination attempt a few minutes after another assassination attempt. I mean they don't usually come that close together from two different parties. Our former First Officer was working for the merchant group Apel. They promised him my ship if he took me out, and unfortunately for him, his attempt failed."

"The Apel group is one of our current challengers. Yes, we need to start taking out some of these challengers to show them who is on top, right Boss?" 42 responds.

"Yes, that is one thing we need to attend to soon as we get back. Ship status and how long before you get to the coordinates I gave you?" Eve inquires.

"All systems go, cleaned up the fires, and repaired the damaged halls where you were ambushed. Should be at the coordinates in about two hours."

"Very good, 42. You will make a fine First Officer. Give yourself a 5% raise. Do you think I should hire someone else to do the accounting or communications? I can or do you think you can handle First Officer duties along with the duties you already have?"

"It is okay, Boss. I am an Android and I can handle it all, so you do not need extra personnel for those other two jobs."

"Very well. Inform me when we arrive at our destination. It will take me two hours to convince the doctor to let me out of this place."

The doctor in the next room replies, "I heard that. You need bed rest and time to heal, Captain. You do not need to be out exploring, adventuring, and being shot up. Besides, you never know when the next assassination attempt will be and so you need to be at full strength."

"I assure you, Doc, I am fine," Eve promises.

"I don't tell you how to captain ships, do I? When it comes to you and this crew's health, my job is to make sure that your well-being comes first. Now the rest of you clear on out of here and let her go to sleep."

The twins and 42 leave the room. Eve begins to rest and falls asleep.

Chapter 4

Two hours pass by and the intercom activates ship-wide. "Action stations! Action stations! Contact made!" 42 announces. Eve awakes and presses her com badge.

"Report!"

"Boss, we have a distress signal coming from an area close to the coordinates that we have arrived at."

"I am coming to the bridge."

"You are so stubborn; it may open up your wound again if you do not watch it," the doctor sighs.

"Just put me on those floating med chairs and I will be okay, Doc. I need to be on my bridge."

"Very well, but I am coming with you to monitor your condition. You do not need a lot of stress right now."

"Fine."

Upon reaching the bridge, Helma and Nelma were on duty along with 42 and Gartooth.

"Status?"

"Picking up a week distress signal coming from the asteroid belt approximately five minutes from this position," 42 informs.

"Hmm…. Sounds like a pirate trap. They use asteroid belts a lot to sucker people in," Gartooth suggests.

"Yeah, that is what I was thinking. Get the stasis net ready for deployment just in case we have any uninvited guests. Also, load those mines up into the mine deployment shuttle." Eve commands. "Move in range of the asteroid belt and launch a class A-probe."

"Launching probe. Readings will begin in 60 seconds," 42 says. "Looks like the asteroid belt is dense, but there is an opening at 98.2 x 36.1 x 52.8 that can fit a ship of our size. The asteroids in the belt consist mostly of non-valuable minerals and ores. Picking up the distress signal, which appears to be an Elemental Empire signal. Coming from within the asteroid belt and the approximate location of the opening, I just mentioned. Probe is too far away to scan for life signs; we need to get closer to the mouth of the clearing of the asteroid belt and I'm not sure from how deep the signals are coming."

"Action stations, code yellow, shields up, prime weapons," Eve announces over the ship-wide intercom. "Move us into the mouth of the opening and launch another probe. Deploy mines on the right side of the opening and activate their cloaking devices. Set the statis net trap to the left after we pass by it. Open the net and have someone standing by to retract it if we have to leave suddenly. That should be sufficient to prevent any surprise visits from behind us."

"Readings from the second probe are coming in.... Appears to be a large asteroid about the size of a small moon approximately five minutes in front of us at a current sub-light speed. The asteroid has building structures on it as well as a large war cruiser on the landing pad close to the structures. Structures appear to be made by the Elemental Empire, but the cruiser is a class 2 undead attack vessel. Coming closer in, there are fighters that have been deployed just drifting in space not moving, approximately 36 undead fighters of different kinds. All ships are inactive and not moving. The facility seems to have no power, no life, or undead activity. I am just picking up a distress signal as far as I can tell," 42 explains.

"What are the undead doing over here in this part of space. This is a long way from Vampire space. Activate condition red. Get a landing party ready with five squads of security officers fully armed with biotech armor; we do not need any of our own turning into the undead. Make sure you pack a lot of flamethrowers and ultraviolet light explosives," Eve orders.

"42, you have command. Make sure you notify me immediately if we have any unwanted visitors. Gartooth, meet me in the cargo bay with our landing party and bring the doctor with us. Bring extra scanners of different types. If this place is some sort of secret facility for the Elemental Empire, then it is always good to be prepared. Must be something special if the undead are interested in it. The Vampires are at war with many empires so, that doesn't mean much. I think only the Reptilian Empire is that only one not at war with the undead, or at least not yet."

Thirty minutes later, the ship sends down two shuttlecrafts. They land next to what appears to be one of the main entrances on the west side of the complex. Twenty fully armed security guards with biotech armor along with Eve, Gartooth, and Dr. Farshe get out of the shuttlecrafts. Eve is still in pain from her injuries, but she is feeling better with the reinforced brace that the doctor put on before they left the ship.

Eve says, "Let's fan out and stay within visual range. Do not go off alone anywhere. Lets go." They walk cautiously to the entrance and go inside. Using the high-beam flashlights on their weapons and their bio-suits, they light up the hallway. They come down to an intersection and see corpses of humans and the undead in all directions. They see the ghastly sight of some destroyed Bone Warriors. Bone Warriors are the undead foot soldiers of the Vampire Empire. They are animated armored zombies that have a highly contagious touch that will turn any living creature into undead Bone Warriors. The humans bodies in the hallway have flamethrowers and are scattered among the half-charred undead. Some of the humans were burned just as the undead were, but several of the others died from hand blaster damage or explosives.

They go down several halls that are filled with offices. They continue onward to another series of small buildings that are research facilities and laboratories. Most of those buildings are empty, except for some of the laboratories that had some dead humans in them.

"Hmm.... Some of these humans in these labs were not killed by the undead. They were killed with objects in the laboratories. Also, I noticed that the undead on the west side were killed in combat. These undead from the north- and east-side labs have no marks on them at all and yet they all are dead," Dr. Farshe reported.

The group goes down some more hallways that lead to a large chamber, the main laboratory. They walk inside this vast chamber to see even more undead corpses mixed in with human remains. None of the bodies seem to have been involved in any type of fighting.

"Man, this place gives me heebie-jeebies," Gartooth remarked.

"These humans over here have no marks on them, and my scanners are not picking up any type of damage or any biological hazard, or at least any known biological hazard. This is a covert laboratory, so there may be some unknown pathogen floating about. Some of the computer systems here still work. I am trying to access information now," the doctor adds.

"Secure this area and do not leave this room. Maybe we can find some valuable information on these computers that we can use."

Grimtooth remarks with a nervous tone, "Look at these vampires over here…it looks like the life has been drained out of them. I didn't think vampires could feed on each other, or why would they? I do not understand. Holy crap, these Bone Warriors have the same markings, what the hell could drain a Bone Warrior?" The entire landing party is beginning to feel very uneasy about this place.

Eve says, "I sense a presence here, a telepath. I can feel the emotions: very chaotic, alone, angry, hungry, confusion. A very powerful mind."

Dr. Farshe says, "This laboratory facility was researching biological weapons according to these records. The experiments included a lot of genetic experimentation with half-breed mixing, most notably with telepathic races and creatures with telepathic abilities. Some of these records are 30 years old. One of the projects named in these records is project Evella."

"What…?" interjected Eve.

"There was a project with your name on it that, according to these records, they were experimenting on reptilian and human telepathy to try and make a more powerful telepath as a means of defense against the undead.

They were trying to make a telepathic slave warrior. The only successful subject was lost about 30 years ago in transit: Subject 37."

"That was me, which means I was created here before I escaped or should I say rescued by pirates," Eve said. "Is there any other mention of me?"

"Query, Evella. While it is doing that, I am downloading all information from this computer onto our ship's computer," the doctor paused. "Yes, there is one other reference to project Evella. It is in another project called Evella 2. This project took some of the DNA from Subject 37 and mixed it with a human male with a high PSI rating. This new formula was introduced into new hybrids that were supposed to give the hybrids the ability to kill vampires and other undead in the same fashion that vampires killed living beings via drainings. In addition, these hybrids also transmitted a very infectious disease to all forms of the undead. Subjects E2-135 and E2-136 were the first successful hybrids to survive the process and who retained the abilities of the project's goal. There were some side effects that gave these two subjects the ability to drain the magic force out of sorcerers whether they were undead or not."

"What that means is they can kill sorcerers in the same fashion they kill vampires by draining the magical force out of them. Undead are primarily given life by magical force, whereas living beings have a different type of life force. Vampires feed off the life force type that living beings have. Telepaths have a different type of life force and thus are the reason for these experimental projects. The researchers basically redesigned a telepath and made it function similar to a vampire but with the requirements of feeding off of magical energy. In simpler terms, a reverse vampire."

"In addition, the telepathic energy that is used to drain magical beings also carries a similar contagion like the undead, except it only infects a host with a magical life force. Basically, it is the undead virus in reverse. This virus is more powerful, though, because it resides in its host even after death for an infinite period of time. That means it is a booby-trapped corpse. Any undead or sorcerer who comes within range or touches the body gets infected."

"Sounds like people playing God, and it looks like one of their experiments decided to kill their masters after they got freed by some unfortunate vampire," Eve states in a not-surprising tone. "I can feel them. They are here, and they are powerful and have no control over their abilities—it is likely a child or children."

"You are the mother of those monsters, so do not forget that. Remember that they were not a willing participant in these experiments," the doctor reminds Eve. "Upload almost complete."

"Good, then we're getting out of here. I will not stick around this place, as I'm getting a bad vibe," Gartooth says.

"Yes, I agree," Eve says.

They begin to move out the same way as they came in and they noticed that the hall that they came down had finally collapsed, so they had to backtrack and go a different way. They decide to travel north. They go up a ways to a four-way intersection and hear some noises coming down the dark hallway, but cannot not pinpoint from which direction. Eve gives Gartooth the signal and gestures to go down the North Hall.

"Why do I always get chosen to go down the creepy hall of doom first?" Gartooth signs. He creeps slowly down the hall with his laser rifle pointed in front. Then suddenly, one of the guards behind him farts very loudly, causing Gartooth to jump backward in fear.

"Really? Seriously?" He looks back and frowns at the guard. The guard just shrugs his shoulders apologetically. Gartooth hears snickering from various sources in the group behind him as he turns to continue. They go down the hallway, slowly checking each room. They discover a large room off to the left, which evidently is the cafeteria. They assume there might be a way out through the kitchen or elsewhere. They enter the cafeteria doorway single file with Eve and Gartooth in front.

Suddenly, two figures come hurling through the doorway on the other side of the cafeteria with glowing blue eyes. They leap up onto a table and hiss with fangs glaring.

"Vampires! Open fire!" Gartooth says. Laser beams start firing at the shadowy figures, as blasters hit the two figures as well as parts of the wall behind them. Neither of the targets seem to be affected by the blasts. One of them launches a lightning bolt, hitting Gartooth in the chest and slamming him backwards into the wall. The other one releases an uncanny screeching sound, and the guards start fighting each other in chaos.

Eve yells, "Get back into the hall now!" as she releases a massive telepathic wind blast that picks up all of the tables and chairs and sends them flying upward, sweeping the two figures along with debris into the wall and making a loud crashing sound. The force was so great it punched a hole in wall leading to the kitchen area. The entire area shakes as the lights flicker on and off. Eve feels the violent rage, confusion, and pain from the two telepaths as they slowly emerged from the pile of rubble. Eve is in the room alone as the others watch on a monitor outside the hall. Eve grabs them telepathically and hoists them up into the air and holds them while trying to focus on suppressing their telepathic abilities. She feels that these two beings are very powerful telepaths who had no discipline, no way to control their powers. She also senses that these test subjects have no idea what is going on and are totally confused. She notices they are wearing metallic collars around their necks—maybe some sort of control device put on by their creators or maybe something that was supposed to inhibit their abilities but is failing to do so. She is straining to hold both of them as they are incredibly powerful minds but very chaotic. She removes the neck devices with her mind. As the devices fall to the floor, the test subjects' chaos and pain subside at a rapid pace. Perhaps their creators did not realize the neck devices did not have the effect they were hoping for. Instead of controlling them, they cause their subjects to go insane.

"Relax, calm down. No one is going to hurt you. It will be okay," Eve said telepathically and sent images of a peaceful and relaxing nature. She looked into their minds and even though their bodies were probably teens or young adult, they seemed to have the education and social skills of a five-year-old. This is probably because their creators were only interested in using them as controllable weapons. They did not even speak a language yet, but they could still communicate telepathically. They calm down and talk to Eve telepathically.

"Where are we? What is this place? I am scared. What is going on? Why are people so mean to us? We are confused."

"We are leaving this horrible place, children. I will protect you from harm. Everything will be okay. No one will be experimenting on you anymore."

"Who are you? Why are you wearing a suit like those mean people?"

"The suit is used to protect me against things that might harm me. You do not need to wear one of these suits because things that can harm me cannot harm you for the most part. I am your mother," Eve flatly states. She looks at them and notices they resemble vampires, but they are different in several aspects. Apparently, they do not need oxygen survive, and walking out in open space does not seem to bother them, much like undead.

"Come with me, children, as we must leave this place at once. It is dangerous to stay here." She gives them a hug and reassures them everything is okay. The two young girls leave the room holding their mother's hands. Out in the hall, the rest of the crew is sitting there watching the monitor out in the hall but not understanding what is going on since most of the conversation was done telepathically.

"Um...so what is up, Boss," Gartooth says, wanting understand.

"It will be okay; these are my daughters, and I am taking them with me. They had some sort of collar on them that I think it was supposed to control them, but instead it was driving them insane. They have the mental development of about a four- or five-year-old. They can't even speak a language yet, which is understandable since their creators were not interested in their educational and social development as they simply wanted a controllable weapon. In my mind, those sadistic bastards got what was coming to them for what they did to my girls and me. Call it poetic justice," Eve said. "I can communicate with them telepathically though."

"Okay, but we will need to keep them separate from the crew until I can confirm that they are not contagious to us. There is one thing I would like to note, they do not register as living beings or undead; instead, they are something else a new sentient life form," Dr. Farshe explains. She looks at Gartooth's bio-armor and sees a huge hole.

"It is okay, Doc. It did not go all the way through as this armor is pretty tough. I could not have taken a second hit—that is for sure. Guess I got lucky. A minor flesh wound," the crocodile winks.

"Back to the ship. Let's go."

After about 30 minutes, the landing party is back on board. Eve's daughters freak out a lot of the crew at first but nonetheless they are taken in. The daughters are placed in bio-suits and moved to Eve's quarters. The doctor starts running tests on them to make sure that they are not infectious to the crew.

Back on the bridge, they are getting ready to move away from the asteroid belt.

"Gartooth, I want you to blow that entire place to dust, including the undead ships, so begin now."

"Yes, Boss. You know how I love to blow stuff up," he commences to pressing buttons. They hear the large explosions below them. They watch on the vid screen after 10 minutes of firing big cannons and unloading some missiles and the entire asteroid is obliterated.

"Helma, let's get out of here."

"Yes, Boss."

After about two minutes, 42 says urgently, "Contact just outside the asteroid belt. Elemental Empire ship signature: it is a battleship, dreadnought class, crew about 3,000, and 35 fighters—they outgun us 10 to 1. The *Telherra*, the Telepath hunter flagship. They are probably responding to the distress signal that we responded to."

"They are probably not going be happy that we blew up their super-secret, black-ops, naughty, naughty laboratory facility," Gartooth remarks, being facetious.

"We are being hailed," 42 warns.

"On vid."

The screen lights up with a picture of a very large black Wolfkin male in a smartly dressed uniform.

"I am General Hurt, the captain of the flagship *Telherra* of the Elemental Empire. You're trespassing in our space. What business do you have here?"

"I am Captain Noctu of the Reptilian merchant vessel...." Eve paused, "Noctu. This is a neutral zone, so how can you claim that we are trespassing? You have no claim to this area of space." She knew that he knew she was lying about the ship's name. She just did not want to say it because it was a name of their main black-op project.

Eve continued, "Besides, there is nothing out here that says Elemental Empire on it, now is there? We are just doing an astrological mineral survey of these asteroids to see if they contain any ores that we might be interested in mining." They knew she was lying. They also knew that she was the one that probably destroyed their lab facility.

"I don't think they are buying that story, Boss," Nelma says, nervously.

"Make sure the mines are active and the status web is deployed and cloaked," Eve says and then presses the reply button to hear the general's reply.

"I think you destroyed our lab facility, and you probably took something that was not yours. I might be able to forgive you for destroying our lab facility if you give me what you took…, Evella," General Hurt demanded.

42 says, "He launching fighters…looks like all of them."

Eve could not think of anything else to delay for more time.

"You have 60 seconds to comply. What is it gonna be, Captain?" Gen. Hurt insisted, with growing impatience.

Eve instructs, "Fire all batteries at the main ship now." She knew they would never let them live no matter what the general said.

Aboard the battleship, orders were flying about.

"General, they are firing on us. Shields are up. Fighters are almost in intercept range. Even though it is a 'merchant' ship, it has firepower, shields, and armor that are impressive for that size of ship. Of course, it isn't a match for a battleship," First Officer Bean informs. Bean was a human about 35 years old; he had been in service for seven years.

"Even if we get the data or whatever they took, they cannot be allowed to live," Councilman Jax demands.

"Yes, I am aware," Gen. Hurt acknowledges. The large black Wolfkin was rather annoyed by the whole situation.

"Now if everyone is done telling me stuff I already know, let me do my job."

Back on Eve's ship.

"Okay, Boss, the fighters just hit our traps. The mines just took out nine of their fighters, and 12 of them are stuck in the status web, and it is draining all their power. They will have no power in about five minutes. The other 14 just engaged us. The shields are holding, but will be gone in few minutes. The small rail guns are firing on the fighters," Grimtooth says.

"Keep hitting the big ship with the big cannons, and fire missiles at the fighters. Nelma, plot a jump course to Reptilian space. We are going to lightspeed as soon as we get out of the asteroid belt. Steer us behind the status nets to their block line of sight using their trapped fighters. Then hook around the net at the last minute and get to our jump point, Helma," Eve commands with authority. Ship-wide intercom activates, "Doctor bring my daughters to the bridge now. Rulu, report to the bridge, and Pura do the same."

"Captain, I have not finished my testing on your daughters yet, so I do not know if they are contagious," the doctor says, using her personal com badge.

"It is not going to matter in a few minutes when we get blasted into a million pieces by that battleship in front of us!" Eve yells in a hurried fashion.

"We have taken out seven of the fighters, but our shields are gone, and we are counting on our armor only right now. Forward rail gun battery on the port side has been hit and is not working," Gartooth says over the exploding noises in the background.

Nelma," Course laid in for the jump, Boss."

"We are at the status net, but the battleship has moved to the front of the opening and is blocking our exit!" Helma says in a panic.

The doctor, the daughters, Rulu, and Pura enter the bridge. Rulu goes over to engineering station and transfers engineering commands to that console. Pura goes to the ship status station.

"Doc, get them out of those spacesuits," Eve blurts out as the ship shakes from an explosion.

Pura says, "We were hit on the port side again in the rail gun ammo holder, all the rounds detonated in the magazine. There is an enormous crater on the port side; levels 13 through 21 and sections 10 through 19 are open to space: 93 dead, almost half the crew."

"The blast took out four fighters and disabled two more. The last one got tossed into the status net from the blast explosion," Grimtooth reported.

"Sub-light and jumps engines still okay," Rulu says.

Helma responds, "Want me to make a run for it and slip around the left side facing the starboard side of the ship to the battleship? We still have armor and guns on that side."

"Yes, when I give you the word. It is going to be a tight squeeze, being that close to their guns we will only have a few seconds to get into jump position. Helma, as soon as we are in position jump, don't wait for my command."

Eve grabs both of her daughters' hands and begins communicating with them about the instructions for her plan. They stand there holding hands and their eyes glowing blue to focus their powers.

On the battleship, a different scene is developing.

"Sir, all of our fighters have been eliminated. It looks like they will try to make a run for it, mostly like using their starboard side facing us as it is the least damaged. They will probably jump if they can make it around us," Bean says with confidence.

"35 fighters! Okay, I am not playing around anymore: open fire with everything we got including missiles," Gen. Hurt commands with a forceful attitude.

"Here they come, firing missiles," Bean says as he presses a button.

Second Officer Ham, "Sir, we are getting a massive energy feedback in our main generator...." The power flutters on the bridge and lights go off and on. "Shields just went offline, Sir...and now the weapon systems."

"What?" the General screams. "Get the backups going now!" he yells.

"Bridge, this is security. We have fighting breaking out on all decks. The crewmen are fighting against each other," the chief of security reported.

"What is the hell is going on? Don't just stand there looking at me, get back to work!" Gen. Hurt roars at the station officers as the lights and panels blink off and on.

Ship-wide intercom is activated on the battleship.

Eve begins to speak," Looks like you have a discipline problem, General... You know that is usually is a sign of poor leadership. I understand that it is hard to find good help these days," She laughs an evil laughter that echoes throughout the ship.

"Mind you, Witch, I going to kill you with my own hands if it is the last thing I do. I am going to hunt you down like the garbage you are. Your mind tricks don't work on me."

"Maybe not, but they do on your officers." Half of the bridge officers point their weapons and begin firing randomly at people.

"Ha-ha-ha-ha!" Eve chuckles aloud. "Councilman, don't think I have forgotten about you and your murdering band of sorcerers. I am going to enjoying watching my daughters suck the life out of each of you."

On the bridge of the Evella, missiles from the battleship coming raining down on the starboard side. Several of them hit, causing more explosions.

Rulu says, "Boss, jump engines hit, and sub-light engines offline."

"On the bright side, we have matching craters on both sides now," Gartooth cleverly inserts.

"Boss, I just lost helm control and we are spinning like a Frisbee. We going to hit that battleship in 90 seconds or so," Helma says with alarm.

"Geez, I got to pee so bad now," Gartooth added.

"Remove command module clamps and begin bridge separation. We are going to detach from the ship and then get as far away as we can," Eve sputters out. She activates ship-wide intercom, "This is the captain. All remaining crewmembers abandon ship, abandon ship!"

"Detaching complete," Rulu says. "Activating Command Module engine and helm control."

"Helm control up. I am steering us away, but this has a small engine's sub-light speed that is lame," Helma says with regret.

Pura says, "Boss, we are are not going to make it out of the blast area in time. The Evella will slam into their reactor core hard because their shields are down."

"Now I really gotta pee," Gartooth squeaks.

Nelma frowns at him and barks, "Seriously?"

"Sorry, I usually just have gas when I am about to die, but I think I drank too much water earlier."

On the battleship, collision alarms are going off.

"Sir, that ship is going to hit us in the reactor core. We need to abandon ship—not that that it will help much."

"Turn the ship some, so we at least have a chance to escape in the pods, you idiot."

"Yes, General."

The General presses a button and abandon ship messages thunder out, as he runs down the corridor heading to the fighter bays. He makes it into the hanger bay of his personal fighter just as a tremendous explosion reverberates throughout the ship. He activates his fighter and begins launching just as a chain of explosions marches down the ship in his direction. He jettisons out of the bay into space and heads full throttle away from the battleship. The battleship begins to break up as a monumental explosion completes the devastation. Large quantities of debris go in all directions, destroying everything in their path.

Both Eve's command module, as well as the General's fighter, are hurled into open space in opposite directions. The electrical systems in both ships flicker off and on. Both are floating in space.

"Wow! That was a heck of an explosion," Rulu says.

"Yeh," Pura agrees.

"Report," Eve requests.

"I need to change my shorts," Gartooth says hesitantly. Helma slaps him on the back of the head.

"I should have everything running in an hour," Rulu assures.

"Until then we will be free flying through space with no controls into the Elemental Empire," Nelma states.

"How far to the nearest Reptilian planet?" Eve questions.

"About 100,000 years without lightspeed, but we will run out of food and water in a week or so, so that is irrelevant," Nelma guesses. "The only planet in range is about 10 days, but it is in Elemental Space."

"Set a course for there, as we don't really have an option," Eve says.

"Okay, will do as soon as Rulu finishes repairs. I will assist. Just hope we don't have any hostiles pop up because we don't have weapons or shields in this thing."

A few hours pass and they make repairs and head off to the nearest planet.

Chapter 5

After traveling into Elemental Space for seven days, the crew is out of food, and very little water is left. Long-range sensors start beeping.

42 says, "Contact bearing 90 degrees starboard. They just dropped out of warp, probably because they detected us. We are not in commercial shipping lanes. What you want to do, Boss?"

"What type of ship is it?"

"Looks like a small Elemental Transport ship, not commercial. The ship's ID indicates a governmental transport of some kind, with about 30 people."

"Okay. Lets play dead; maybe they will try to board us."

"Just life support barely on…well, that actually isn't false, ha-ha," Helma laughs.

"Pass out the weapons."

"Roger that, Boss." Gartooth starts handing the weapons.

"They are heading this way," Pura says. A few minutes pass and they hear the other ship trying to attach to the airlock.

"They will come up to the bridge first, so lets wait in the storage space downstairs that is near the airlock. When they come in, they will go down the other hall and up the stairs to the bridge. We will slip onto their ship, de-attach the airlock connector, and trap them here. Then we'll take over their ship. They will probably send over most of their security since it is a small vessel, and we can trap them on our ship."

They run down to the storage space and wait. After a few minutes, they finally see seven people who look like security guards and a couple of leader types. Eve senses magic, so one of the leaders must be a sorcerer. She can feel the overwhelming urges of her daughters, as they smell food come through the doorway.

"Patience, my pretties. Not that one, but there is probably one on the ship that you can eat so just wait," Eve assures her daughters. She sees the intruders go down the other hall.

"Let's go," Eve whispers. They pile into the airlock and go across. When they emerge on the other side, there is a human male about 25 years old standing in robes and guarding the door. The young sorcerer, probably an apprentice, is caught off guard, but before he can react the daughters have plunged their claw hands into his chest and back. They began to suck his life force out of him in a frenzy. His face and body shrivel up like a dried prune as the girls snap him into two pieces in the same fashion as dogs fighting over food. The others freak out over what they just witnessed. They back away from them in fear. Eve feels the satisfaction her daughters felt.

"It's okay guys. They only eat sorcerers and undead, so relax. They are just as hungry as we are, and they just eat different food. Let us move," Eve states as she de-attaches the airlock bridge. She then destroys the controls so they cannot be activated again.

"Here is an access panel. I am plugging into the computer, getting the maps for the ship, and um...this is a prison ship: 16 prisoners and 14 crew. Seven are on the other vessel, and four flight crew and two others are still here, considering we just killed one," 42 says.

"Let's go up to the bridge first and get control before they figure out they have been duped."

They head up to the bridge. Upon entering the bridge, the flight crew figures out something is wrong but it is too late. Eve grabs all five of them using telekinesis.

"Bind them. Gartooth, Pura, and Doc, find the last one. 42, figure out how to fly this thing. Helma and Nelma, take navigation and helm stations," Eve commands quickly.

"I am linked with the ship computers. Fortunately, they did not have time to lock us out. I am changing all the command codes to ones that only we know. We have complete control of the ship now."

"Good. Back us away from the other ship, and blow our ship up using their weapons."

"Roger that," 42 says.

Helma moves the ship away and fires all weapons at the other ship. The ship is destroyed.

"Plot a course back to Reptilian space and let us get out of here."

Nelma says, "Plotted."

Rulu says, "Jumping to light speed now. Should be home in 14 days."

Downstairs on the cell levels, Gartooth's party sees some cells with prisoners in them and then spots a human guard who bolts down some stairs at the other end of the hallway. They begin to chase after him. They go down a couple of flights of stairs to the bottom level and then an alert begins blaring.

"Danger! Prisoner escape! Isolation cell red!" The message continues to cycle over and over again.

Gartooth goes down the corridor with the others following behind him. They come down to two doors at a 'T' intersection. One door is red and one yellow.

"Special cells that look like they are magical. And that peckerwood we are chasing decided to let something out," Gartooth presses his com badge and says, "Boss, the dude we were chasing let something mean and nasty out of a special cell down on the bottom level."

42 replies, "Looking it up on the prisoner roster. Says 'Classified, level one clearance needed to access.' Sorry, can't help you."

"Bah."

"Um, I think I know what was in that cell," Doc says peeking down the other hall. The others come and look as well.

"Yeh...I am pretty sure it is an arachnid."

"You think?" Gartooth stares down a hall filled with huge spider webs. "I hate arachnids. Haha, looks like we don't worry about that human." As he knocks on the humanoid cocoon in the center of the webs, he also notices that a corpse has been sucked dry.

"Yeh, the webs harden when contact is made—a silicon-based material. Keeps the food fresh until the arachnid is hungry," Doc says.

"I could have gone all day without picturing that in my head," Pura says with a queasy stomach.

"There are two types of arachnids: sorcerers and warriors. Sorcerers cast webs to catch food, and warriors can go invisible at will and enchant weapons like swords and then track down and kill their prey. It appears this one is a sorcerer, I will inform the Captain," Doc states. She presses her com badge.

"It appears we have a sorcerer arachnid running loose down here, Captain."

"Okay. I am on my way, so wait there." Minutes later, Eve appears at Gartooth's location.

"The ship's diagram shows a cargo area down this corridor and to the left. Let us proceed with caution." They to go down the hall and turn to the left and creep through the door that leads into a large cargo chamber. It is filled with huge webs that cover the entire cargo bay. The party is standing there in astonishment at the size and density of these webs.

"I sense something, but it is not magical, not a sorcerer. It is a familiar presence telepathic in nature. Not picking anything up on sensors with these hand-held devices, but I feel it," Eve whispers quietly. She goes into the cargo bay slowly and cautiously.

"I know you're in here, as I feel you. I sense your fear. I am not here to harm you. I feel your pain," she says transmitting a telepathic message. She receives images of an arachnid in a laboratory being tortured and experimented on in a horrific manner.

"42, recall that lab data from your memory banks and do a search for arachnid experiments," Eve says.

"Yes, Boss," he says using his com badge. "Yes, it appears they captured a young female arachnid warrior and did many experiments on it. They made it undead and used its physiology as a baseline for the disease that was created to destroy the undead. They also injected PSI enzymes from your DNA sample to see what would happen to a non-telepath. The creature is immune to the undead disease but is still a carrier. The PSI injections had some unusual effects on the arachnid, such as being able cast webs like a sorcerer arachnid. The eyes were altered as well. The subject has the ability the fire energy beams from its eyes that cause catastrophic damage as well as area-of-effect knockback to things that are close to the target. Her eye beams are similar to the main cannon on a battleship. An eye device was created to modulate and control this effect and placed on the creature. I would advise proceeding with caution as this ship was not designed to take hits from a battleship cannon."

"Understood," Eve, acknowledges.

"Geez, you gotta to be kidding me—freaking laser beam eyes?" Gartooth says with concern as he and the rest of the party back out of the room in fear. Eve has the same concerns but stands there in the middle of the cargo bay in the midst of all the webbing. She switches her sensor scanner to translator mode and a setting for reptilian-arachnid.

"I know that you are hurt and scared. We have captured this ship, and the people who did this to you have been captured or destroyed. The laboratory that you were in was also destroyed. We are here to help you, not to harm you. Please trust me. I can remove the control collar around your neck, but I cannot do it unless I can see you," Eve reassures. "The sorcerer with the controller for your collar has been destroyed as well."

A bluish-purple arachnid appears, hanging from the ceiling webs. She has a human female's torso with black spider legs and a large red hourglass on her stomach. She is wearing a visor over her eyes and has a control collar around the neck. She also has short bright orange hair on her head with matching orange lips with protruding fangs.

"There you are…you are so pretty," Eve says as she unlocks the collar, and lets it fall to the ground. "Come down here and let me get a look at you." The spider slowly comes down the webs and moves toward Eve. Eve gestures with her hands to come forward. She could still feel the fear coming from this poorly treated creature. Eve walks up to the arachnid.

"You are truly beautiful. What is your name?" Eve asks.

"Gothica," she replies.

"That is a good name for an arachnid. I like your hair," Eve says, running her fingers through the short orange hair. Eve could feel the fear dissipating somewhat from Gothica.

"I want you to meet some friends of mine. They are little scared of you, but it is okay." Eve gestures for the rest of the group to come inside. The doctor comes inside and the others follow shortly at a slower pace—not too thrilled about meeting in arachnid.

"My name is Doctor Farshe Mezeenabark, but calling me 'Doc' is okay. Pleased to meet you, Gothica. I never actually met one of your race. Are you hurt in any way?"

Gothica hears the word doctor and suddenly fear takes over.

"Gothica, Doc is not like those people in that laboratory. She is not going to harm you. She actually keeps me and the crew from getting sick or hurt. She just wants to make sure you are okay. This is Gartooth and Pura."

"Um, high. Can I go to the bridge and check on the prisoners?" Gartooth says, just looking for any reason to leave.

"Sure," Eve frowns at Gartooth.

"Hi, there, I think you're an adorable spider-person," Pura says with a wink. She notices Gothica looking at her jewelry. "Oh, you must like jewelry? Here, take this necklace as it matches your hair." She offers her the necklace. Gothica hesitantly accepts the gift. Pura helps her put it on.

"Pura, stay with Gothica for a bit, if you don't mind. I need to get back up to the bridge," Eve says. "Doc, come on."

"Sure, I think we will get along just fine, cat and spider—we are both predators, ha-ha. Besides, I want to paint her nails orange to match her hair. I wish I had four arms—that is so cool," Pura says, getting out her nail kit. "I never leave home without it," she giggles. Gothica feeling a lot more comfortable and begins laughing with Pura as she begins painting the nails of one of her four hands.

As Eve and the Doc walk up to the bridge, Eve says, "Just remember that she was in a laboratory being experimented on so lay off the poking and prodding if all possible. I know you are curious just like all doctors are, but around her you are probably going to have to explain everything that you do, including touching her or poking or whatever. The poor creature has been tortured enough."

"I know. I'm just exciting about having an arachnid on board, even though she is undead. I do not think she really understands what being undead means. Everyone is going to hate her. Being an arachnid is hard enough. What about your two daughters? They are worried about being around an undead, are they? A word of caution, this particular undead is not one that your daughters would want to feed off of as it will probably kill them. Just make sure they understand that. This is a mutant undead. Also, I noticed she still has many injuries; she will need to feed on live subjects to heal all of the damage that was done to her. She is probably not susceptible to ultraviolet light like the regular undead are."

"I will inform my daughters when I get up to the bridge."

As they continue down the corridor and walk into the bridge, she sees the five prisoners bound up and sitting on the floor.

"Take the prisoners down to the cargo bay, Gartooth."

"You mean down where the….?"

"There is more space," Eve interrupts, "One at a time."

"Yes, Boss." He does not like this assignment.

Eve says telepathically to Gothica, "Gartooth is bringing some food for you. They are some of the people who captured you."

When Gartooth brings the first one down into the cargo room, the prisoner begins to scream when she sees the arachnid. Gartooth tosses the human female into the webs and exits the room to get the next one.

Gothica sees the prisoner and scurries over to the struggling prey. She wants to feed but hesitates and turns around to Pura.

"Whatcha waiting for? I don't mind. Eat and remember I am a cat and we cats eat the same way. There is nothing to be ashamed of" Pura reassures her.

"I am not used to eating in front of people," Gothica says. The human is screaming in terror by this time.

"Go ahead."

After hoisting the body up with her four arms, the arachnid plunges her fangs into the human. The body goes limp after a few minutes, and Gothica feels much better as her wounds heal.

"I feel much better now. I guess I will wrap the others up in a cocoon and eat them later."

"Yeah, after I eat, I just feel sleepy. Come back over here and let us finish painting your nails. They will look so cool, and they going to match your hair." They both giggle.

Back on the bridge, everyone is feeling more at ease now that they are on the way home. Everyone is eating food from the galley.

"We have plenty of food for us, but I am not sure were going to have enough food for all those prisoners," Doc says, trying to calculate food consumption.

"Let us get rid of some of the prisoners then. Pull up the prisoner roster and see what we got," Eve says unconcerned.

42 pulls up the list on the main vid screen.

"Looks like we have 16 prisoners. Eight are telepaths on charges of being a telepath. Four are captured telepaths or collaborators. One is a political prisoner. Three are just psycho serial killers who need to be killed."

"Keep the telepaths and the collaborators alive. That has to be the most stupid law I ever heard of: Being a criminal just because you are a telepath. I mean, seriously, that is retarded. We will let the telepaths and the collaborators off at home world. Do you have enough food to include the political prisoner?"

"Should be able to manage."

"Okay then. The serial killers will be fed to Gothica."

"The political prisoner is also a sorcerer."

"Really? That is interesting," Eve says with intrigue. "I am gonna go down and talk to our political prisoner. You know what they say, 'the enemy of my enemy is my friend.'" She disappears down the corridor. A few minutes later, she walks by the force field doors of the cells on level 3. She comes to the appropriate cell according to the prisoner manifests.

"So, Archibald, it says here you're a political prisoner, which is odd for a sorcerer to be a political prisoner in the Elemental Empire."

The male human replies, "I don't know who you are and what you are doing on the ship, half-breed…whatever. None of your business why I am here."

"My, such an attitude, and here I was thinking about releasing you—guess not."

"Are you pirates looking for a ransom? Unfortunately, my brother will not pay anything for my release because it was I who tried to overthrow him and assume my rightful place."

"So you are a failure. A failed sorcerer. You look lonely. I can arrange for some company for you. I will send two of my girlfriends down here to keep you company."

"I don't need any slutty girlfriends to come down here."

"They will be here in a few minutes."

Eve sends a telepathic message to her daughters to come to cell 18. After a few minutes, her starving girls come around the corner.

"Enjoy, my sweeties," as Eve drops the force field. The girls pounce on the arrogant sorcerer and began draining all of the life force out of him. They rip him to shreds as his screams echo down the hallway.

"Nothing like fresh sorcerer on the table, or I should say arrogant bastard?"

All three of them head back up to the bridge.

"I think I will name you, Xaqu and Chaca Noctu, my daughters. Remember you cannot eat Gothica because she is poisonous to you. She has my blood running through her just as you do. In fact, I think I will adopt her and she will be your step-sister. So you will need to get along with each other," Eve says telepathically. "I need to get some education for all three of you and learn some languages."

After a few days passed, they enter Reptilian space. Eve activates the main vid screen.

"Contact Fartan Balltail."

A male snake man appears on the screen.

"Well, how's my favorite client? Have not heard from you in a while," Fartan says snidely.

"Don't you mean 'money pit' that you suck funds from?" Eve says with no sarcasm in mind. I am gonna need a bunch of documents drawn up. Going to need birth certificates for two, which are for my daughters 17 and 18, and citizenship papers as well. Will also need some adoption papers for an arachnid female, age 17, that I found with the citizenship papers. Also, need some papers made up for a salvaged ship with the following serial numbers; it is an elemental transport ship. I am sending over the details now."

"Looks like you have been busy. I can make all the documents for my usual fee, but the arachnid is gonna cost you four times as much and lot more bribing."

"Do not give me that crap! I will give you double for the arachnid and not a platinum bar more or your wife finds out about your mistress."

"Okay, calm down. I accept your terms."

"I will contact my office on home world and have it transfer the money to you. Make sure you have all those ship documents filed at the port by the time I arrive at the landing pad. The ship still has elemental identifying markers painted on it. I will change the transponder now to the new salvage title identification number. Just tell the port officers that I will be painting the correct numbers after I land. Make sure you do it quickly. I do not need the ship to be confiscated due to improper paperwork. I have already lost an expensive ship this week not to mention couple of hundred good workers."

"Also, contact the Consortium consulate and tell them I need papers for 12 telepathic refugees and get reptilian work visas for them as they will be working for me. I will transfer the information on them to you shortly."

"I also need you to make up a couple of shell corporations and make them complex enough so it will be difficult for anyone doing research to find out who owns the companies. I am planning on some hostile takeovers and company purchases and I do not want anyone to figure out exactly what I am doing until it is too late. Also, I know that in your profession you run across a lot of seedy characters. I need one of your contacts from the black market, if you can arrange that. I'll give you a hundred platinum bars, 50 for you and 50 for the contact just for setting up the meeting."

"Sounds like you've got big plans, and I can smell the money now," Fartan says, already spending the money in his head before anything has even happened.

"I think when they created the saying 'Lawyers are a bunch of slimy snakes' they were thinking about you, Fartan," Eve remarks.

The snake man responds," Why, thank you, My Lady," trying to figure out if that was a compliment or an insult.

After a few days, they enter the port at Hoshan and touch down.

"Yes, I see your lawyer filed all the papers on this ship, but he didn't pay the docking fee or the penalty fee for not have the correct ship identification number painted on the vessel," the port supervisor insists.

"That is a bureaucracy for you," Gartooth says.

"Okay." Eve gets out the currency transfer pad from her vest and pushes some buttons. "There, that should do it," she sighs.

"Okay, and here is a package your lawyer left," the supervisor says as he hands her a box. She opens up the box full of passports and other documents. There is also a note in there from Fartan.

"The Consortium consulate will have the rest of your documents."

"Okay, guys, take a month-long vacation. I have some things to attend to, and I added bonuses for everyone for this hardship we have been through. I am going to be working on getting us a new ship. 42, I need you to check on the status of our other ships and the funds we have available to buy a new ship before you take off on vacation," Eve says to the crew.

"Thanks, Boss" they say as they depart on their separate ways.

Doc says, "Don't think it is a wise idea to allow Gothica to walk around in the city, as she is undead."

"We do business with arachnid merchants here in the home world. They even have a consulate here. Granted there are not very many of them here and they are a rare sight, but they are hardly a disruption. As far as being undead, the only reason you think that is because you know she is undead. But look at her: she looks like any other arachnid as her coloring has not changed or anything. You said yourself she is a mutant undead. I mean they eat the same things and the same way whether they are alive or undead. The sun has no effect on her and trust me no one will know. Besides, she will probably walk around invisible most of the time because she shy."

"Hmm....That is true. You know me, I am just a worry wart."

Eve chuckles," That is the truth."

"I will do more research on arachnids while I am on vacation. I will read a lot of books and stuff, as I am a curious person."

"That is fine, Doc. I will call you and we'll do lunch sometime next week."

"Sure." The Wolfkin waves goodbye as a taxi hovercraft appears and scoops her up. About that time, a rather large hovercraft appears in front of Eve. It is a luxury model with all the bells and whistles. A human chauffeur gets out and goes to the other side to open the door.

"Hi, Henry, I see you been keeping my prized limousine in good condition while I have been gone. I do not have any baggage this time around as I lost my ship, but I'm going to go shopping with my daughters. Say hello to Xaqu and Chacu and my adopt daughter, Gothica," Eve announces.

Henry is alarmed by the sight of Gothica who has changed her legs into two humanoid legs while still having four arms.

They all got in the eight-seater hovercraft that had vid screens and other cool gadgets.

"Take us down to the market center. Stop at the Giuliana's store first, Henry."

"Yes, ma'am."

"Okay, girls, stay close to me and do not wander and no eating people, okay?" Eve felt that was odd thing to have to say, but chuckled inside nevertheless.

"Gothica, people are not use to seeing arachnids on this planet, so they might stare at you, but do not be alarmed. If you just want to walk around with us, being invisible is fine."

"Okay. I am nervous anyway."

"We are nervous, too," the sisters say telepathically to Gothica and Eve.

"Well, if anyone messes with us, we will just eat them," Gothica says with sarcasm and winks at the two sisters. All three of them laugh. Eve frowns at them, but then laughs.

"No eating people…young ladies," Eve says with a smirk. Gothica, being a warrior arachnid, has the ability to enchant magic weapons, so she can enchant some items and let her step-sisters drain the magic for food.

The first stop they make is at a clothes shop. They enter the rather large boutique and start trying on clothes. Gothica stays invisible and follows them. Eve still sees Gothica even when she is invisible. The doctor said that the more contact she has with the three girls, the more she will pick up their traits or another phenomenon because they are mutant versions of her DNA. The girls might also pick up some of their mother's traits.

"So put the ones you like into that basket and I will pay for them. Those outfits you are trying on now are cute, so just keep those on, and I will buy them, too."

They picked up their packages and got back in the large limousine. They headed down the street to an arachnid vendor Eve remembered seeing before. They pulled up in front of a small shop and went inside. Gothica decided not go invisible this time. Upon entering the store, they saw two arachnid shopkeepers wearing beautiful silk clothes. There were arachnid clothes of all types and sizes hanging from the walls and turnstiles. The beautiful coloring of the clothes was one of the fascinating things about this little store. Exotic jewelry and metal weapons, daggers, throwing items, and bows were also hanging in a different parts of the shop.

"Greetings. I am Vosha and this is my assistant Higja," Vosha said, speaking for both female arachnids.

Eve says, "Hello. Nice shop you have here. These are my daughters, Xaqu and Chaca, and step-daughter, Gothica."

"Don't get many arachnid customers in these parts, unfortunately. Most of my sales are jewelry and weapons. You have beautiful daughters. I think we can accommodate Gothica very well here."

"Good because she needs some clothes and other stuff."

Vosha looks Gothica over.

"She is pretty big, even for an arachnid. Must be warrior class with those muscles. I have some fashionable arachnid clothes and some warrior armor in her size." She signals to her assistant to fetch the merchandise. The assistant comes back with some boxes, and all of ladies, including the sisters, start putting clothes on Gothica. She picks about nine outfits and three sets of arachnid warrior armor that fit her. She also gets some shoes and combat boots especially designed for arachnids as well.

"Every good warrior needs some weapons. Let us go and look at these weapons over here and see what you like," the shopkeeper suggested.

Gothica examines some of the weapons and swings a few.

"I like the swords, but I need four of them."

"All of our weapons are made in fours for obvious reasons. Here are the other two. These are made out of Osmiridium metal, which is harder than diamonds and is extremely hard to break and very easy for a warrior to enchant. Very expensive at 100 platinum bars each. They come with matching sheaths that snap onto your armor."

"We will take them," Eve says.

Gothica takes the swords and holds all four in the air and starts to mumble. "*Ney cha fer do asa metu*" and the swords light up with magical flames. The feat was surprisingly impressive to all the ladies there—not something many get to witness. They clap in excitement. She enchants her armor, too.

"Now I know you ladies would want some jewelry to go with all your new clothes." Walk over to the jewelry section. Xaqu spots a snake staff that she likes and asks her mother if she can have it.

"Yes, dear, you can get it. I think it will look great with your outfits."

"I can enchant it for you, too, Xaqu," Gothica says. Xaqu's face is filled with happiness. They continue to try on jewelry for a couple of hours before they leave.

"Take us home, Henry."

"Yes, ma'am."

They arrive home, and Eve shows them around and assigns each of them their rooms. Then they stay up talking, playing games and, of course, laughing a lot. The girls have never had this much fun in all of their lives.

Chapter 6

After spending a couple of days at Eve's home, the door chimes. Henry, who is the butler as well as the driver, walks down the hall and answers the door. There is a tall skinny Android in yellow and chrome metal with triangle eyes standing there.

"Greetings, I am assistant 123, I work with the consulate for the Consortium. I have been instructed by my government to invite Evella Noctu to the consulate for a meeting with our administration."

"I will inform the Madame promptly, wait here." Henry walks down the hall and knocks on the door.

"Ma'am, someone is here from the Consortium consulate and has requested your presence at the consulate to have a meeting with their administration."

"Okay, Henry, tell them we will be there within 30 minutes."

"Excellent, ma'am." Henry walks down the hall back to the front door and tells the representative the lady will be there within 30 minutes. The Android leaves. Just as Henry begins to walk down the hall again, he sees Eve emerge from her room.

She says, "Bring the hovercraft around the front. I need to get the girls up and dressed."

"Excellent, ma'am." Henry disappears outside and goes to the garage. Eve goes to the back part of the house and wakes up the girls and tells them to get dressed as they are leaving in 10 minutes. After a few minutes, the group of four women emerges out of the front door and climbs into the hovercraft waiting for them. After a quick 10-minute flight downtown, they come up to the Consortium consulate and land at the drop-off point at the front gate. Henry pulls the hovercraft around to where the other limousine drivers are waiting at the consulate. The four women go through the main entrance after being scanned for weapons. They continue through the courtyard into the main building. They see androids all over the place, some of them working as employees and some trying to get different types of documents from the government.

"That is a whole lot of Androids, but the Consortium has about 20 billion citizens, I'd guess," Eve remarks to her daughters. They take a number and sit down among the hundreds of androids and other people trying to get service. A few minutes later, an Android comes up to Eve.

"Lady Noctu, you do not have to wait here. Please come with me. The Creator is expecting you. Follow me."

Eve thought to herself, *who is the Creator?* They got up and followed the Android down a few halls and onto an airlift that was going down. Eve notes that the airlift has no floor buttons on it and thought this is very odd. After descending downward for several minutes, the airlift stops and opens up. They get out and turn left and go down the long hallway. In this hallway, there are soldier Androids walking through the corridors and posted at each of the doors. A big sign on the wall indicates the restricted area in several languages.

They walk down to the end of the hall and take a right. Then they go down another long hall and take a left. The door opens up into a large grand hallway with two big doors at the end. The grand hallway is lined with soldier Androids who are heavily armed. They go down to the end of the hall and the two large doors open slowly and they walk inside a vast chamber that has the Consortium symbol in the middle of the floor. The chamber is empty of people but does have pictures of various places and a huge vid screen that covers most of the north wall in front of them.

"Wait here," the Androids instruct and then leaves the room in the same manner that they came in. After the Androids leaves, there is a pause of silence. A couple minutes later, two big glowing eyes appear on the screen.

"Greetings, Evella Noctu," an ominous voice says with a slight echo ringing. "Thank you for coming as we have much to discuss you and I. I am Dracabardillous, created and leader of the Machine People or better known as the Consortium."

"Yes, I believe we have met before. You contacted me."

"Indeed I did."

"What are you doing here in this place. This is just a consulate."

"I am in many places all over the universe at the same time—multitasking, if you will. Consortium space is vast and extends to many regions and galaxies. Thousands of worlds have our citizenry. It might be hard for you to understand this concept. I am an energy being with different limitations than what you can probably comprehend."

"I see. What do you want from me? I am just a mere mortal woman."

"On the contrary, you are not simple at all. In fact, that is why you are here speaking to me now. You and your daughters will play a fundamental role in bringing this region of space under control and unified as one entity. That is one of the reasons I saved your daughters."

"Um, I think you've got me mixed up with someone else. I am not a hero by any stretch of the imagination. And what you are talking about is a little above my ambitions in life or should I say way above my goals in life."

"The hero is not what is needed to consolidate the intelligent life forms in this region of space. A leader is needed who would be willing to make the tough decisions with wisdom and not heart. Deciding to sacrifice thousands to save millions or millions to save billions, and not everyone can make these types of decisions. Sometimes things need to be done that are not ethically correct but the ends justify the means."

"Well, I am not following you, as this seems to be above my head."

"To put it in terms that you can understand, you are the only one in this region who can conquer or persuade all of the empires in this area of space to become under one rule, your rule."

"Whoa…back up there, buddy. I know you've got the wrong person now. I definitely do not want to be some Grand Empress over the galaxy. I can just imagine all of the enemies I would have trying to kill me on an hourly basis. I think I will pass."

"You already possess great personal power; it is highly unlikely that anyone knowing this would challenge you. You do not need armies to get what you want. You just need intelligence, wisdom, and tactics. You have the intelligence already, and I can help you with wisdom and tactics. I will also educate your daughters and teach them many languages, history, science, mathematics, politics and how to use their telepathic abilities on a master level. I can show you what powers you possess and how to use them skillfully. We have technology that can accelerate the education process."

"That sounds intriguing, but why are you doing this? With your vast military and your personal power, you can quickly consolidate this area of space."

"Unfortunately my resources are being used in other galaxies far away from here against invaders who are vastly more powerful than anything you can imagine—even I have limits. This is why I chose you to help with this. There will be a time in the future where invaders such as the ones I am fighting now in another part of the universe will come here. This region must be prepared for that day by being unified as one instead of several squabbling empires fighting against each other as they are now."

"Hum…that sounds very scary. Very well, let us proceed then. About this educational technology, how fast does it work exactly or should I say how does it work?"

"Works similar to the computer to download information into your brain and sections at a time will take about 30 days. I will also show you how the telepathic concepts that you will learn are used in practical applications. Also, I have four special telepathic suits created for each of you that will graft to your body. They are thin and lightweight pieces. They absorb magical and energy attacks and convert them into PSI energy. The more you are attacked, the stronger you get, and the more powerful your telepathic abilities are. You will not need to activate devices for shields any longer, as you can generate your own PSI shield from mere thought. The more PSI energy you have, the stronger the force shield becomes. These suits will help you achieve your goals. This is the best I can do for you under the circumstances."

"That will be adequate and thank you for your help. I can hear your thoughts. Thirty days that will be fine. Okay, girls, follow me to the educational room. We are going to be there for a while." They leave the room and go to a different level where there are a bunch of chairs and a large chamber with wires connecting to a huge headset. They sit in the chairs, put the helmets on, and lay back. The helmets activate and start the education modules.

⁂

Over a month passes by as Eve and her daughters learn many things during this period. They also practice many of the skills they have discovered that they possess.

"Yes, most impressive indeed, Lady Eve. Gothica is the finest example of an arachnid warrior I have ever had the pleasure of training. Most warriors master one or two weapons during their lifetime and she has mastered three," Weapons Master Jazrath says as they both stand watching Gothica practice on the weapons range.

"That is awesome," Eve says with enthusiasm.

Jazrath yells out, "Show your mother what you can do, Gothica." The Weapons Master is a male arachnid transported here by the Consortium to train Gothica. She runs through some moving targets and whips out her four swords and slashes the objectives with blinding speed and accuracy.

"Excellent," Eve shouts and claps in approval.

Next, the arachnid hurls several throwing daggers from a bandolier of daggers into several targets with pinpoint precision. Both of the observers clap vigorously. Then she moves down to the rifle and hand blaster range. The range activates and five targets that shoot up in the sky. Gothica quick draws four hand blasters out of their holsters and rapidly fires all of them, easily dispatching all five targets, then twirls her blasters and shoving them back in their holsters. She winks at her mother in rodeo fashion.

"Ha-ha, you show-off. You just need a cowboy hat now!" Eve teases. All three of them laugh. An Android comes on the practice field and walks over to Eve in an efficient manner. It was one of the educational instructor Androids working with her other two daughters.

"Greetings, Lady Eve. I am here to give you the progress report you requested. Xaqu has shown an extremely high aptitude for engineering, most notably in weapons design. Chaca, oddly enough, also has a great skill in engineering. She has very impressive designs for starships. They both can speak Arachnid, Elemental, Wolfkin, Reptilian, and Katin at a master level. They scored very high on the IQ tests, just as you did. One other thing we discovered is who their father is—if you want to know."

"Yes, I want to know."

"The lab use DNA extracted from Capt. Zach Blem when he was in captivity."

Eve was surprised by this news and was unsure how to react to it. He probably has no idea he has two daughters, but was he going accept them, as they were, mutant experiments?

"Where is Capt. Blem currently?"

"He came in this morning from the Consortium home world. Right now, he is at the consulate in our temporary lodging."

"Thank you for your information."

"No problem, my lady, good day." The Android walks off and disappears into a hovercraft waiting for him on the other side of the field.

"Is she about done for today?"

"Yes, this is her last day with me, I cannot teach her any more than she has learned," the Weapon Master says, with a hint of sadness.

"Don't worry. We will stay in contact with you. She doesn't have a lot of arachnid friends."

"Yes, I look forward to talking to her again. Here she comes."

"So I guess we are done for today?"

"Yes, this is your last day, so make sure you keep in contact with me, young lady. I want to hear about all of your adventures. I am an old person who does not get out much. Contact me whenever you get to the arachnid space. We will go out and do some shooting or something."

"Oh yes, definitely, and thank you for all of your help and I would never have done this well on my own," Gothica says and leans over and hugs the Weapons Master.

Eve says, "Okay, Hun, lets go."

As they depart from the field, they see Henry waiting with their limousine. They climb into the limousine and dart off into the distance toward the consulate. After a short flight, they get out and go inside the consulate. The consulate is busy, as a lot of travelers are going in and out. The pair goes down to the lower levels to check up on Xaqu and Chaca.

After searching for a few minutes, they find Xaqu in a room that appears to be an assembly area for Androids or is perhaps a maintenance bay. There are two other Androids in there with her. They are standing and looking at what she has created.

Eve and Gothica go over to see what all the commotion is about. As they walk up, they see a sleek, shiny chrome female Android who looks very similar to Eve.

"She looks like me!" Eve says with amazement.

"Yes, Mother. I was working on a new Android design and I decided to make it look like you. Doesn't it looked neat?"

One of the Androids says, "Your daughter is very talented not just with weapon design but with Android design as well. I believe this is the most advanced Android that has ever been constructed to date. She took the concept of the suits that we designed for you to wear and altered it to create a material that absorbs cosmic radiation such as solar power and converts it into energy that can recharge an Android's battery. With this new exoskeleton, an Android can run indefinitely without ever having to recharge. Your daughter's grasp of chemistry and electronics is astounding."

"I am so proud of you, daughter," Eve says and hugs her tightly.

"You are just about to turn it on to see if it works…knock on wood," Xaqu says, nervously hoping not to fail in front of her mother. "Here we go." She flips on the switch in the back of the neck. There is some noise inside of the Android and it appears to be active. Suddenly, the eyes began to glow as a large bolt of energy arcs from the computer they are standing next to hits the Android.

"Hmm…very interesting design," Draca says with intrigue. "Sorry for hijacking your Android, as I have been observing your progression and was curious as to how it turned out. I was looking at the schematics yesterday and wondered how the practical application would function. You have done very well, Xaqu. You have created a next-generation Android with this design and my citizens are in your debt. It is only appropriate that we call this the Xaqu model. I would like to use this prototype model for myself, if you do not mind—unless your mother objects, as after all it might make her feel uncomfortable having a metallic Eve walking around."

"Ha-ha, I don't mind. It is uncanny how much it resembles me. You are very good with art, it would appear, Xaqu."

"Thank you for your kind words, ma'am. I do not mind if you keep the prototype as they can always make more and would like to keep working on perfecting the design, if you do not mind. I like making androids."

"Certainly, by all means. I know this maintenance bay is not exactly a research and development laboratory, but I will give you a computer that links to our R&D department on home world that will give you access to more stuff you can experiment with. They always welcome gifted minds like yourself, especially when it comes to developing Androids."

"Now that would be excellent," Xaqu says with excitement. The Empress leaves the room.

"Let us check on her sister and see what she is up to," Eve suggests.

"She was practicing her telepathic abilities earlier and I am not sure what she is doing now," Xaqu says and turns to Gothica. "I look like a real mercenary or pirate with all those weapons."

Gothica smiles, "Yeah, just need an eyepatch or parrot."

"Or a cowboy hat, then you can be a space cowboy," their mother interjects. They all laugh as they walk out the door and go down some halls looking for Chaca. They walk into a room where Chaca is training with another telepath. They stop and sit in the observation seats above the training area. Chaca is about to be tested.

The female snake instructor says, "You must be able to find your targets under any circumstances by using all of your senses because there may be a time where one or more of your primary senses, such as sight or hearing, may be impaired. This test we going to blindfold you and make you use your hearing to guide you to your targets. Begin!"

Some balls start flying around the room in random directions. Chaca is blindfolded and is concentrating to release a lightning bolt in the general area that would take out the balls. Two more come flying toward her from behind and she ducks and fires a wideband electrical charge that strike both targets. A bunch of balls come flying out at one time from her left side and she hear those and launches a large cone of ice shards that fly into that direction and destroy all of the targets.

The instructor says, "Splendid, Chaca. I see your mother is here and so we are done for the day. Put all the gear up while I talk to your mother." She walks over, sees her other pupil, Xaqu, and gives her a hug.

"Your daughters are very gifted and are the strongest telepathic students I have ever had. They are very smart, and so I guess they take after their mother."

"Perhaps, but I give them a lot of credit for being their own selves."

"I am sorry that I never got to work with you, Eve. Empress Dracka wanted to work with you directly, and besides, I think your abilities are far beyond anything I could teach you."

"Yes, Dracka is definitely an odd one to figure out, but she is very knowledgeable when it comes to telepathic abilities, though."

"Your daughters have basic telepathic communication abilities like all telepaths have along with some telekinesis abilities. These are not as strong as yours are, though. Xaqu can manipulate intelligent beings on a mass scale like I have never seen before. She has mass chaos mind, mass charm, and mass hallucination and fire attacks. In contrast, Chaca can control the weather with a massive gust of wind and electrical and cold attacks as well."

"That is good to know. Thank you for working with them and you've done a marvelous job."

"Thanks for letting me work with them. Now, they are done as far as what I can teach them."

"I will stay in touch with you. You have been a good mentor to them," Eve smiles.

Chaca finishes putting her training materials away, and then she joins her mother and her sisters.

"You did well today, Chaca, and I am very proud of you," Eve says with honesty. She gives Chaca a hug. Okay, girls, wait in the limousine outside. I have to make a detour to another room here to meet with someone. I will be up there in a little bit. You can watch the vid for news or other programs until I come up there and meet you. Just tell Henry to wait and I will be there in a minute."

The girls disappear and go upstairs and out the front door where Henry is waiting and get into the limousine. Eve goes up a few levels and gets off the airlift and starts searching the halls try to find the temporary quarters. After wandering around for a bit, she finds a hall with the sign above it that says temporary quarters. She walks over to the front desk and says, "Excuse me, is Capt. Zach Blem staying in one of these rooms?"

The Android replies, "Let me check one second…yes, I have him registered here."

"Could you contact him for me and tell him Eve is waiting at the front desk?"

"Sure, one second." The Android presses a few buttons: "Capt. Blem, there is a woman named Eve waiting for you. Okay, I will tell her." The Android disconnects and says, "He says to go up to his room; he is in unit 43." Eve nods and goes down a few halls until she sees room 43 and knocks on the door. A few moments later, Zach answers the door.

"Well, hello, Beautiful. What brings you to a slimy dump like this?" Zach says with sarcasm.

Eve pushes inside the room and begins hugging and kissing him. They have not seen each other in a couple months, and she is making sure he knew it.

"How's my stud been?" Eve says with curiosity.

"I have been fine, Sweetheart. What have you been up to?"

"Just boring merchant stuff, nothing exciting."

"Why do I doubt that. You just don't want me to worry. I think I might have been missing you too much. I thought I saw an Android in the lobby who looked just like you. I must be losing my mind," Zach laughs.

"But, of course, my evil Androids were getting ready to take over the universe," Eve smiles and winks while running her hand through his hair. If he only knew, she thought to herself.

"Sit down for a minute. We need to have a serious conversation."

Zach could sense the mood changing, so he went and sat next to Eve on the sofa.

"So it is up?" Zach inquired.

"I found that laboratory where I was created. I went there and found some other discoveries that you might find interesting because they have to do with you. I destroyed the entire place after I obtained a few items. Remember when the telepath police captured you?"

"Yes."

"They took a sample of your blood, several samples, as a matter of fact. They shipped them off to that secret lab where they were doing experiments with telepathic DNA that had high PSI ratings."

"I do remember them taking blood samples and never knew what they were for."

"Well, they combined my DNA with your DNA and created two half-breed girls—our daughters. They were doing experiments on them that involved torturing them."

"What…that is horrible…well, I don't mean the part about the daughters, I mean the torturing part. What happened to them?"

"I saved them and they are with me. I only found out yesterday that you were their father. They are very intelligent and have extremely powerful telepathic abilities. They also have other skills, for example, they are both good engineers. Their names are Xaqu and Chaca. They are very well educated and speak many languages. And you did see the Android who look like me created by Xaqu. She has a gift for creating Androids."

This was a lot for Zach to absorb all at one time. He sat there motionless and not knowing how to react to this news. Then there was a pause of deadly silence when no one spoke.

"Well, that is a lot for me to absorb at once. On the bright side, it appears that we can make babies, so that means we get to play Doctor more often, right?" Zach says in a humorous manner to break the tension that appeared to be building up.

Eve laughed and said, "So you are okay with this? They are 17 and 18 years old."

"Of course, I am okay with it, why would not I be? Two awesome daughters with the woman I love. I am just kind of upset that we did not get to play Doctor to make them the old-fashioned way…wink-wink, nudge-nudge."

"You are so silly sometimes," Eve giggles. "There is more."

"Oh my goodness, there is more?"

"Yes. There was a young female arachnid warrior who was being experimented on in that laboratory as well. They injected her with some of my PSI enzymes to see what would happen to a non-telepath with a high dose of my enzymes. It had a couple of unusual effects on her, and she survived only because of her high regeneration ability that she got because they made her undead."

"Well, that is really creepy, as that place sounds more like a dungeon than a laboratory. Is she okay? You don't see arachnids too often in this part of space."

"She is fine; I adopted her as my daughter. She is a very skilled warrior with weapons. She is my little space cowboy. I was hoping you would accept her as she is."

"Sounds intriguing for sure," Zach states. "I was going to wait to do this later, but now seems to be a more appropriate time." He pulls out a small box and opens it, and there is an enormous ring made out of diamonds. "Eve, I love you, and I want to marry you, no matter what."

Eve was caught off guard, not expecting this scenario in any fashion. A moment of silence took hold in the room. Zach was getting worried that she was not responding in any way.

"Yes, of course, I will, Darling." Eve hugs and kisses him. "Oh, I forgot our daughters are waiting out the limousine. Need to go, are you coming?"

"Sure, let's go. I want to meet my children, even my adopted one."

They collected themselves and went outside and got in the limousine with the girls.

"Xaqu and Chaca, this is Zach Blem. He is your father."

They are both surprised. Eve could feel their excitement. Even Zach could feel their excitement.

"My, my, I have such beautiful daughters and never knew it. Your mother has said that you are smart as well. I always knew that we would have beautiful children," Zach says as the girls blush.

"They are a little shy at first, but they will grow on you. Speaking of shy, Gothica you can stop hiding now. She is super-shy around new people."

Gothica slowly appears and sits next to Xaqu.

"Wow, invisibility, and super cool. I like your orange hair, it's neat. I guess instead of high-fives it will be high-20s with you. I wish I had four arms, then I would get so much more accomplished. You are a cute little arachnid," Zach remarks, trying to lighten the mood. They all giggle.

"Zach has asked me to marry him so all of you will officially have a father," Eve says with much joy.

Xaqu says, "Oh, that is fantastic. When is the wedding, Mom?"

Chaca asks, "Can I be a bridesmaid?"

Gothica says, "I've never been to a wedding this will be this fun. Can I bring my blasters or is that inappropriate? A real father was something I have never had before and I have always wanted one."

"We will work all that stuff out later, girls," Eve assures them. "Henry, go to the house."

After a short trip, they pull up in front of Eve's house. They all get out and start toward the door. Zach notices a reflection from a shiny object out of the corner of his eye. He turns his head and sees the end of a rifle protruding out of the bushes next door. At that exact moment, the sniper fires as Zach lunges forward to block the beam from hitting Eve while at the same time yelling, "Ambush!"

Zach is hit in the side and knocked backward into Henry, who was just closing the door of the limousine. In a split second, laser fire was coming from all directions—too many to count. The girls instantly put up force fields surrounding themselves.

"Henry, get him in the car and get out of here," Eve yells out as heavily armored men come running around both sides of the house and from across the street firing different types of weapons at the four women. The force fields absorbs the energy beams and make their shields stronger. Realizing the energy beams are having no effect, the leader yells out, "Change to projectile weapons!" The complete front side of Eve's house has huge blaster holes in it.

Eve sends out telepathic instructions to the girls. Xaqu decides to make the mercenaries on the right side of them her friends. Suddenly, all of them start firing at the other men in front. She has mass charmed them. Chaca releases a huge cone of dagger-shaped ice shards that fly straight at the large group of men in front of them. The ice daggers slice through the armor they are wearing as if they were butter. They scream in agony as they fall to the ground.

On the left side, there are about 20 or so mercenaries rushing from various positions and firing their weapons. Henry got out of there with Zach, fortunately. Gothica turns to the right and changes into arachnid form with her spider legs sprouting out into the ground. She blankets the entire right side with a gargantuan size web that encases most of the soldiers who were advancing. She dodges the bullets from the few who were left as she pulls out her blasters and fires back with all four guns blazing.

Eve turns around when machine gun fire starts coming from her rooftop. She sees men tossing explosives. She grabs the devices in the midair with telepathy and sends the explosives back to where they came from. A huge explosion rips up large portions of the roof, causing it to collapse along with the men standing on it.

Eve sees four armored hovercrafts coming in their direction above the top of her home. Their twin-cylinder rail guns are firing through her home at her and the girls. Large-caliber bullets rip through the house as they fly over it firing down at Eve's location. Eve lifts her house from its foundation and crashes it into two of the armored hovercrafts. The entire mesh of hovercrafts and house parts gfall to the ground and began sliding off the back side of the edge of the hill. As a ball of flame crashes down to the bottom of the hill, it causes more explosions.

Gothica turns around after dispatching the few stragglers over on her side and sees the hovercrafts coming. She activates her visor and releases a horrific green energy blast from her eyes that roars across the scene and hits the nearest hovercraft, obliterating it completely.

Xaqu has her small charmed army shooting at the last hovercraft. Chaca releases a massive lightning bolt that hits a hovercraft's engine and sends it thundering down on the house below where it erupts into a ball of fire.

Eve scans the scene and looks for more enemies to kill. The area is filled with unfathomable carnage and destruction.

"Are you okay, girls? Anybody injured?" Eve asks.

"We are okay. Who would send this many people to kill us? What do you want me to do with these guys that I have charmed?" Xaqu inquires.

"I don't think any of them are leader types. They probably do not know who hired them as grunts, but we can try to find out. Bring them over here and I will scan their minds."

She scans all 11 soldiers, but they are all foot soldiers and have no idea who their employer is.

"They do not know. They also have no marks on them that indicate which company they are from, which is unusual, and they humans. A human mercenary unit is not something that you see in the Reptilian Republic, but I suppose is not unheard of. As far as what to do with them, these mercenaries they knew the risk—kill them all. Make sure there are no survivors. We do not want people knowing how powerful we are."

"You think this was one of the merchant groups we are at war with?"

"No dear, a low-level licensed company would not have the resources or even spend the resources on an attack of this magnitude against my company that has only a level 8 license. Apparently, I have created an even greater enemy that appears to be unseen. That is okay. I will find out who it is, and they will learn just who they are screwing with. They attacked us and shot your father and they will pay. This is only the beginning, even if I have to hunt them down to the ends of the universe."

⋏

A tall snake man dressed in leather and high boots with blasters on both hips walks down a hall decorated with elegant paintings. He stops and knocks on a large door with a gold handle.

"Enter." A deep-voiced person says with firmness.

The snake man enters the large, elaborately decorated conference room with a big table and several large chairs made of gold and velvet. There is a huge chair facing the other way and looking out the window with someone sitting in it. The snake man can only see a hand and goblet from his vantage point.

The figure in the chair says with impatience, "Well?"

"Sir, the Strikeforce was annihilated and the targets suffered no damage. There was one person who was collateral damage in her party and some other people in surrounding homes."

"Hmm…I suspected as much. I guess my informants were telling the truth. Dracka does not invest time on people who are insignificant."

"Do you wish to send another Strikeforce, Master?"

"No, it is not necessary. The Strikeforce was a test to see if Lady Eve is worth my time. She may be exactly what I am looking for as well as her three daughters. Who was injured or killed?"

"Our sources say her boyfriend who others say may be the father of Eve's daughters."

"That could cause some complications. Did he die or is he still alive?"

"He is in intensive care and looks like he should pull through, at least they are hoping."

"Very well. I will have to figure out solutions to either scenario. Keep me informed."

"Yes, Master."

"Now get out."

The snake man leaves the room.

The person sitting and looking out the window says in a firm tone, "So you really think she is the one, eh?"

"Yes, I do," The arachnid Weapon Master appears after shedding his invisibility.

"Then get that lame excuse of a pirate to report to me."

To be continued in Episode 2